# The Big Book of
# Short Stories

*Some other books by Dick King-Smith*

BACK-TO-FRONT BENJY
BLESSU
CLEVER DUCK
DINOSAUR SCHOOL
DUMPLING
GEORGE SPEAKS
THE GREAT SLOTH RACE
THE HODGEHEG
A HODGEHEG STORY: KING MAX THE LAST
HOGSEL AND GRUNTEL
HUGE RED RIDING HOOD
THE INVISIBLE DOG
THE JENIUS
JULIUS CAESAR'S GOAT
THE MAGIC CARPET SLIPPERS
MR POTTER'S PET
POPPET
ROBIN HOOD AND HIS MISERABLE MEN
SMASHER
THE SWOOSE
THINDERELLA
TRIFFIC: A RARE PIG'S TALE

# DICK KING-SMITH

# The Big Book of Short Stories

*Illustrated by Amanda Harvey*

Published by the Penguin Group
Penguin Books Ltd, 27 Wrights Lane, London W8 5TZ, England
Penguin Putnam Inc., 375 Hudson Street, New York, New York 10014, USA
Penguin Books Australia Ltd, Ringwood, Victoria, Australia
Penguin Books Canada Ltd, 10 Alcorn Avenue, Toronto, Ontario, Canada M4V 3B2
Penguin Books India (P) Ltd, 11 Community Centre, Panchsheel Park, New Delhi – 110 017, India
Penguin Books (NZ) Ltd, Cnr Rosedale and Airborne Roads, Albany, Auckland, New Zealand
Penguin Books (South Africa) (Pty) Ltd, 5 Watkins Street, Denver Ext 4,
Johannesburg 2094, South Africa

On the World Wide Web at: www.penguin.com

Penguin Books Ltd, Registered Offices: Harmondsworth, Middlesex, England

*A Narrow Squeak and Other Animal Stories* first published by Viking 1993;
published in Puffin Books 1995
*Philibert the First and Other Stories* first published by Viking 1994; published in Puffin Books 1996
*The Ghost at Codlin Castle and Other Stories* first published by Viking 1992;
published in Puffin Books 1994

This edition published by Viking 2001
1

Text copyright © Fox Busters Ltd, 1992, 1993, 1994
Illustrations copyright © Amanda Harvey, 1992, 1993, 1994
All rights reserved

The moral right of the author and illustrator has been asserted

Printed in Britain by Omnia Books Ltd, Glasgow

British Library Cataloguing in Publication Data
A CIP catalogue record for this book is available from the British Library

ISBN 0–670–91240–9

# Contents

A Narrow Squeak and Other
Animal Stories                                    1

Philibert the First and
Other Stories                                   109

The Ghost at Codlin Castle
and Other Stories                               203

# A Narrow Squeak and Other Stories

# Contents

A Narrow Squeak      5

The Excitement of Being Ernest      25

Norty Boy      47

The Clockwork Mouse      57

The Happiest Woodlouse      77

Use Your Brains      91

# A Narrow Squeak

'Do you realize,' said Ethel, 'that tomorrow is our Silver Wedding Day?'

'So soon?' said Hedley in a surprised voice. 'How time flies! Why, it seems but yesterday that we were married.'

'Well, it isn't,' said Ethel sharply. 'You only have to look at me to see that.'

Hedley looked at her.

She seems to have put on a great deal of weight, he thought. Not that she isn't still by far the most beautiful mouse in the world, of course, but there's a lot more of her now.

'You have certainly grown,' he said tactfully.

'Grown?' snapped Ethel. 'And whose fault is that, pray? Anyone would think you didn't know why I'm blown out like a balloon. Goodness knows what sort of a father you will make.'

'A father?' said Hedley. 'You mean . . .?'

'Any time now,' said Ethel. 'And I'm starving hungry, Hedley. Fetch us something nice to eat, do. I could just fancy something savoury.'

She sighed deeply as her husband hurried away. Was there ever such a mouse, she said to herself. *So* handsome, but so *thick*. Let's hope he doesn't walk straight down the cat's throat. I wouldn't put it past him, and then there won't be any

Silver Wedding.

A mouse's life is, of course, a short one, fraught with hazards. For those that survive their childhood, Death looms in many shapes and forms, among them the cat, the poison bait and the trap, and mice have learned to commemorate anniversaries in good time. 'Better early than never' is a favourite mouse proverb, and Ethel and Hedley's Silver Wedding was to be celebrated twenty-five days after their marriage.

If they were lucky, they would go on to a Pearl, a Ruby, a Golden, and, should they be spared to enjoy roughly two months of wedded bliss, to a Diamond Wedding Anniversary. Beyond that, no sensible mouse cared to think.

If only Hedley was more sensible, Ethel thought as she lay, uncomfortably on account of the pressure within her, in her nest. Not that he isn't still by far the most beautiful mouse in the world, of course, but he's so accident-prone.

Hardly a day passed when Ethel did not hear, somewhere about the house, a thin cry of alarm, indicating that Hedley had just had a narrow squeak.

He goes about in a dream, she said to herself. He doesn't *think*. Surely other mice didn't stand in the path of vacuum cleaners, or explore inside tumble-driers, or come close to drowning in a bowl of cat's milk?

In fact, Hedley was thinking quite hard as he emerged from the hole in the skirting-board that was the entrance to their home, and prepared to make his way across the kitchen floor.

'A father!' he murmured happily to himself. 'I am to be a father! And soon! How many children will there be, I wonder? How many will be boys, how many girls? And what shall we call them? What fun it will be, choosing the names!'

This was what Ethel had meant when she said that Hedley did not think. Her

thoughts were very practical and filled
with common sense, and she was quick
to make up her mind. By contrast, Hedley
was a day-dreamer and much inclined to
be absent-minded when, as now, he was
following up an idea.

He had just decided to call his eldest
son Granville after a favourite uncle,
when he bumped into something soft and
furry, something that smelt, now that he
came to think of it, distinctly unpleasant.

The cat, fast asleep in front of the

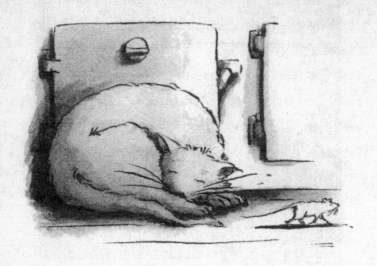

Aga cooker, did not wake, but it twitched its tail.

With a shrill cry, Hedley ran for cover. The larder door was ajar, and he slipped in and hid behind a packet of Corn Flakes.

The noise he had made reached Ethel's ears, and filled her mind, as so often over the previous twenty-four days, with thoughts of widowhood. It also woke the cat, who rose, stretched and padded towards the larder.

'Not in there, puss!' said its owner, coming into her kitchen, and she shut the larder door.

Hedley was a prisoner.

For some time he crouched motionless. As happened after such frights, his mind was a blank. But gradually his thoughts returned to those unborn children. The eldest girl, now – what was she to be called?

After a while Hedley decided upon Dulcibel, his grandmother's name. But then suppose Ethel did not agree? Thinking of Ethel reminded him of her last words. 'Fetch us something nice to eat, do,' she had said. 'I could just fancy something savoury.'

Hedley raised his snout and sniffed.

This little room, in which he had never been before, certainly smelt of all kinds of food, and this reminded him that he was himself a bit peckish. He began to explore the larder, climbing up on to its shelves and running about to see what he could find. I'll have a snack, he said to himself, to keep me going, and then I'll find something really nice to take back to Ethel.

Much of the food in the larder was in cans or packets, but Hedley found a slab of fruit cake and some butter in a dish and a plate of cold chips. At last, feeling full, he hid behind a row of tins and settled down for a nap.

Meanwhile, back at the nest, Ethel was growing increasingly uneasy. He must have had his chips, she thought, and our children will be born fatherless. She was hungry, she was uncomfortable, and she was more and more worried that Hedley had not returned.

'Oh Hedley, how I shall miss you!' she breathed. '*So* handsome, but so *thick*.'

While Hedley was sleeping off his huge meal, the larder door was opened.

'Just look at this cake!' a woman's

voice said. 'And these leftover chips! And the butter – little footmarks all over it! We've got mice.'

'Put the cat in there,' said a man's voice.

'Can't do that or it'll be helping itself too.'

'Well, set a trap then. And put some poison down.'

And a little later, the larder door was closed again.

Hedley slept the whole night through. He dreamed of happy times to come. In his dream, his handsome sons and his beautiful daughters had grown old enough to leave the nest, and he was taking them on

a conducted tour of the house. Then boldly he led them all, Granville and Dulcibel and the rest, and their mother too, through the cat-flap and out into the garden. 'For we will picnic,' he said to them, 'in the strawberry bed. The fruit is ripe and the weather exceedingly pleasant.'

'Oh Papa!' the children cried. 'What fun that will be!'

'But are you not afraid of the cat, Hedley dear?' said Ethel nervously.

'Ethel, Ethel,' said Hedley. 'When have you ever known me afraid of anything?' and the children chorused, 'Oh, brave Papa!' . . .

He woke from his dream with a number of other possible names for the impending family in mind – Eugene, Tallulah, Hereward and Morwenna were four that he particularly fancied – when he suddenly remembered with a sharp pang of guilt that Ethel was still unfed.

I shall get the rough edge of her tongue, he thought, and he looked about for a tasty item of food, small enough for him to carry.

He climbed down to a lower shelf and found something which had not, he was sure, been there before.

It was a saucer containing a number of little blue pellets, and beside it there was an opened packet. Had Hedley been able to read, he would have seen that on the packet was written:

MOUSE POISON, KEEP AWAY FROM DOMESTIC ANIMALS

As it was, thinking how unusual and attractive the blue pellets looked, he took a mouthful of them. She'll love these, he thought, such a pretty colour, and he ran down to the floor of the larder only to find the door shut. Bother, thought Hedley. How am I to get out of this place?

He was considering this problem in a half-hearted way, for part of his mind was still occupied with names – would Annabel be better than Morwenna? – when his nose caught a most exciting smell. It was cheese, a little square lump of it, conveniently placed on a low shelf.

The cheese was in fact on a little wooden platform, an odd-looking thing that had a metal arm and a spring attached to it, but Hedley, busy deciding that after

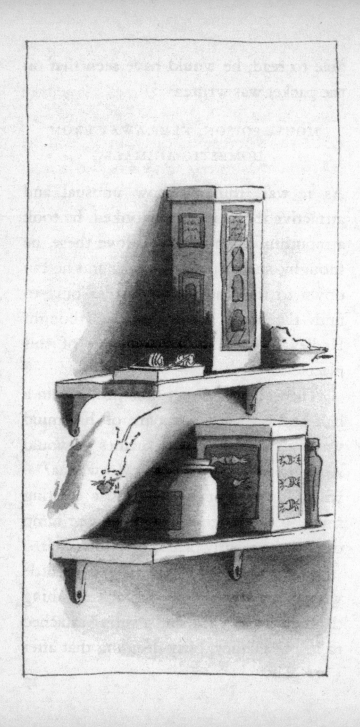

all he preferred Morwenna, did not stop to think about this. It's Ethel's favourite food, he said to himself, and just the right size for me to carry back, and he spat out the little blue pellets and ran to grab the cheese.

Whether it was his speed or whether the trap had not been lightly enough set, Hedley got away with it.

SNAP! went the trap, missing him (though not by a whisker for it cut off three of them), and Hedley gave, through his mouthful of cheese, a muffled squeak of fright.

'Listen!' said the woman's voice, and 'You got him!' said the man's, and the larder door was opened.

For once Hedley did not day-dream. He streaked across the kitchen floor and into his hole, the lump of cheese clenched in his jaws.

Ethel regarded him silently from the nest.

Hedley dropped his burden before her.

'Sorry I'm late,' he panted. 'I got held up. Here, it's Farmhouse Cheddar, your favourite. How have you been?'

'Busy,' said Ethel shortly.

'Busy?' said Hedley.

'Yes,' said Ethel.

She attacked the cheese hungrily, while Hedley lay and got his breath back. Funny, he thought, she looks slimmer than she did yesterday. As slim, in fact, as the day we met, and what a meeting that was! I remember it as though it were yesterday . . .

'Hedley!' said Ethel now, licking her lips as she finished the cheese. 'You do know what day it is, don't you?'

'Wednesday, I think,' said Hedley. 'Or it may be Thursday. I'm not sure.'

'Hedley,' said Ethel. 'It is our Silver Wedding Day.'

'Oh!' cried Hedley. 'I quite forgot.'

Typical, thought Ethel. He'd forget his head if it wasn't screwed on.

'I have a present for you,' she said, and she rose and stood aside from the nest.

In the middle of a comfortable, warm bed, made out of flock from a chair lining, and feathers from an eiderdown, and a mass of newspaper scraps, lay six fat, pink, naked babies.

'Three boys and three girls,' she said. 'Neat, eh?'

Oh! thought Hedley. What could be neater! Granville and Dulcibel, Eugene and Tallulah, and Hereward and Morwenna.

'Oh, Ethel dearest,' he said. 'I have no present for you but my love.'

At these words Ethel's annoyance melted away. What a fine-looking mouse he still is, she thought, not a grey hair on him. In fact, he looks no older than he did at our wedding, twenty-five long days ago.

Hedley sat in a daze, gazing at the babies.

Then he said, 'Oh Ethel! To think that you did this all on your own! You're so *clever*!'

And you're so *thick*, thought Ethel fondly, but out loud she said, 'Oh Hedley, you are *so* handsome!'

# The Excitement of Being Ernest

The first thing that struck you about Ernest was his colour. If you had to put a name to it, you would say 'honey' – not that pale wax honey that needs a knife to get it out of a jar, but the darker, richer, runny stuff that drips all over the table-cloth if you don't wind the spoon round it properly.

That was the colour of Ernest's coat, and the second thing about him that was remarkable was the amount of coat he carried. He was very hairy. Body, legs, tail, all had their fair share of that runny-honey-coloured hair, but it was Ernest's face that was his fortune, with its fine beard and moustaches framed by shortish, droopy ears. From under bushy eyebrows, Ernest looked out upon the world and found it good. Only one thing bothered him. He did not know what kind of dog he was.

It should have been simple, of course, to find out. There were a number of other dogs living in the village who could presumably have told him, but somehow Ernest had never plucked up the courage to ask. To begin with, the other dogs all looked so posh. They were all of different breeds, but each one appeared so obviously well bred, so self-assured, so upper class, that Ernest had always hesitated to approach them, least of all with a daft question like, 'Excuse me. I wonder if you could tell me what sort of dog I am?'

For that matter, he thought to himself one day, I don't even know what sort of dogs they are, and then it occurred to him that that would be a much more sensible question to ask and could lead perhaps to the kind of conversation about breeds in general where one of them might say, 'I'm a Thingummytite, and you, I see, are a Wotchermecallum.'

So after he had helped to get the cows in for morning milking on the farm where he lived, Ernest trotted up to the village to the gateway of the Manor House – an imposing entrance flanked by fine pillars – and peered in under his bushy eyebrows. Standing in the drive was the Manor House dog. Ernest lifted his leg politely on one of the fine stone pillars, and called out, 'Excuse me! I wonder if you could tell me what sort of dog you are?'

'Ich bin ein German Short-haired

Pointer,' said the Manor House dog, 'if dot is any business of yours.'

'Oh,' said Ernest. 'I'm not one of those.'

He waited expectantly to be told what he was.

'Dot,' said the German Short-haired Pointer pointedly, 'is as plain as der nose on your face,' and he turned his back and walked away.

Ernest went on to the Vicarage, and saw, through the wicket-gate, the Vicar's dog lying on the lawn.

'Excuse me,' said Ernest, lifting his leg politely on the wicket-gate. 'I wonder if you could tell me what sort of dog you are?'

'Nom d'un chien!' said the Vicar's dog. 'Je suis un French Bulldog.'

'Oh,' said Ernest. 'I'm not one of those.'

The French Bulldog snorted, and though Ernest waited hopefully for a while, it said nothing more, so he walked down the road till he came to the pub.

The publican's dog was very large indeed, and Ernest thought it best to keep some distance away. He lifted his leg discreetly on an empty beer barrel and shouted across the pub car-park, 'Excuse me! I wonder if you could tell me what sort of dog you are?'

'Oi'm an Irish Wolfhound,' said the publican's dog in a deep, rumbly voice.

'Oh,' said Ernest. 'I'm not one of those.'

'Bedad you're not,' said the Irish Wolfhound. 'Shall Oi be after tellin' yez what sort of a dog ye are?'

'Oh, yes please,' said Ernest eagerly.

'Sure ye're a misbegotten hairy mess,' said the Irish Wolfhound, 'and it's stinking of cow-muck ye are. Now bate it, if ye know what's good for you.'

Ernest beat it. But he wasn't beaten.

He paid a call on a number of houses in the village street, repeating his polite inquiry and receiving answers of varying degrees of rudeness from a Tibetan Terrier, an American Cocker Spaniel, a Finnish Spitz and a Chinese Crested Dog. But none of them volunteered any information as to what kind of animal he himself was.

There was one house left, by the junction of the road with the lane that led back to the farm, and standing outside it was a dog that Ernest had never seen before in the neighbourhood. It looked friendly and wagged its long, plumy tail as Ernest left his customary calling-card on the gate.

'Hello,' he said. 'I haven't seen you before.'

'We've only just moved in,' said the friendly stranger. 'You're the first dog I've met here, actually. Are there a lot in the village?'

'Yes.'

'Decent bunch?'

Ernest considered how best to answer this.

'They're all very well bred,' he said. 'I imagine they've got pedigrees as long as your tail,' he added, 'like you have, I suppose?'

'You could say that,' replied the other. 'For what it's worth.'

Ernest sighed. I'll give it one more go, he thought.

'Straight question,' he said. 'What sort of dog are you?'

'Straight answer, English Setter.'

'English?' said Ernest delightedly. 'Well, that makes a change.'

'How do you mean?'

'Why, the rest of them are Chinese, German, Tibetan, Irish, American, Finnish – there's no end to the list.'

'Really? No, no I'm as English as you are.'

'Ah,' said Ernest carefully. 'Then you know what sort of dog I am?'

'Of course,' said the English Setter. 'You're a Gloucestershire Cow-dog.'

The hair over Ernest's face prevented

the Setter from seeing the changing expression that flitted across it, first of astonishment, then of excitement, and finally a studied look of smug satisfaction.

'Ah,' said Ernest. 'You knew. Not many do.'

'My dear chap,' said the Setter. 'You amaze me. I should have thought any dog would have recognized a Gloucestershire Cow-dog immediately.'

'Really?' said Ernest. 'Well, I suppose any English dog would.'

'Yes, that must be it. Anyway you'll be able to compete with all these pedigree chaps next week.'

'Why, what's happening next week?'

'It's the Village Fête.'

'Oh, I don't go to that sort of thing,' said Ernest. 'I've got too much work to do with the cows.'

'Quite. But this year there's a new attraction, apparently. They've just put the posters up, haven't you seen?'

'Didn't notice,' said Ernest.

'Well, there's one stuck on our wall. Come and have a look.'

And this is what they saw.

## VILLAGE FÊTE
### Saturday June 15th
By kind permission, in the grounds
of the Manor House

---

*Skittle Alley*
*Coconut Shy*
*Cake Stall*
*Jam and Preserve Stall*
*White Elephant Stall*
*Hoopla*
*Wellie-throwing Competition*
*Guess the Weight of the Pig*
*Grand Dog Show*

'But that's no good,' said Ernest. 'With all the pedigree dogs in the village, the judge will never look twice at me.'

'But that's no good,' said Sally. 'With all the pedigree dogs in the village, the judge will never look twice at Ernest.' Sally was the farmer's daughter, and she was looking at another of the notices, tacked on the farm gate.

'Oh, I don't know,' said her father. 'You might be surprised. Have a go. It's only a bit of fun. You'll have to clean him up a bit, mind.'

So when the great day dawned, Ernest ran to Sally's whistle after morning milking and found himself, to his surprise and disgust, required to stand in an old tin bath and be soaked and lathered and scrubbed and hosed, and then blow-dried with Sally's mother's electric drier plugged in to a power point in the dairy.

'He looks a treat,' said the farmer and his wife when Sally had finished combing out that long, honey-coloured coat. And he did.

Indeed when they all arrived at the Fête, a number of people had difficulty in recognizing Ernest without his usual covering of cow-muck. But the dogs weren't

fooled. Ernest heard them talking among themselves as the competitors began to gather for the Dog Show, and their comments made his head drop and his tail droop.

'Well I'll be goshdarned!' said the American Cocker Spaniel to the Tibetan Terrier. 'Will ya look at that mutt! Kinda tough to have to share a show-ring with no-account trash like that.'

And, turning to the Finnish Spitz, 'Velly distlessing,' said the Chinese Crested Dog. 'No pediglee.'

'Ma foi!' said the French Bulldog to the Irish Wolfhound. 'Regardez zis 'airy creature! 'E is, 'ow you say, mongrel?'

'Begorrah, it's the truth ye're spakin,' said the Irish Wolfhound in his deep, rumbly voice, 'and it's stinking of soap powder he is.'

As for the German Short-haired Pointer, he made sure, seeing that he was host for the day, that his comment on Ernest's arrival on the croquet lawn

(which was the show-ring) was heard by all.

'Velcome to der Manor, ladies and gentlemen,' he said to the other dogs. 'May der best-bred dog win,' and he turned his back on Ernest in a very pointed way.

'Don't let them get you down, old chap,' said a voice in Ernest's ear, and there, standing next to him, was the friendly English Setter, long, plumy tail wagging.

'Oh, hello,' said Ernest in a doleful voice. 'Nice to see you. I hope you win, anyway. I haven't got a chance.'

'Oh, I don't know,' said the English Setter. 'You might be surprised. Have a go. It's only a bit of fun.'

He lowered his voice. 'Take a tip though, old chap. Don't lift your leg. It's not done.'

Suddenly Ernest felt much happier. He gave himself a good shake, and then when they all began to parade around the ring, he stepped out smartly at Sally's side, his long (clean) honey-coloured coat shining in the summer sunshine.

The judge examined each entry in turn, looking in their mouths, feeling their legs and their backs, studying them from all angles, and making them walk up and down, just as though it was a class in a Championship Show.

When her turn came, he said to Sally, 'What's your dog called?'

'Ernest.'

From under bushy eyebrows, Ernest looked out upon the judge.

'Hello, Ernest,' the judge said, and then hesitated, because there was one thing that bothered him. He did not know what kind of dog Ernest was.

'You don't see many of these,' he said to Sally.

'Oh yes you do. There are lots about.'

'Lots of . . .?'

'Gloucestershire Cow-dogs.'

'Of course, of course,' said the judge.

When he had carefully examined all the entries, he made them walk round once more, and then he called out the lady of the Manor with her German Short-haired Pointer. When they came eagerly forward, trying not to look too smug, he said, 'I've finished with you, thank you.'

And he called out, one after another, the Chinese Crested Dog and the Tibetan Terrier and the American Cocker Spaniel and the French Bulldog and the Irish Wolfhound and, to finish with, the Finnish Spitz, and said to each in turn, 'I've finished with you, thank you.'

Until the only dogs left on the croquet lawn were the English Setter and Ernest.

And the judge looked thoughtfully at both of them for quite a time before he straightened up and spoke to the owner of the English Setter.

'A very close thing,' he said, 'but I'm giving the first prize to the

Gloucestershire Cow-dog,' and he walked
across to the Vicar whose job it was to
make all the announcements on the public
address system.

'Well done, old boy,' said the English Setter. 'It couldn't have happened to a nicer chap.'

'But I don't understand,' said Ernest. 'How could I have won? Against all you aristocratic fellows that are registered with the Kennel Club, and have lots of champions in your pedigrees?'

'Listen,' said the English Setter as the Tannoy began to crackle and the voice of the Vicar boomed across the gardens of the Manor House.

'Ladies and gentlemen! We have the result of our Grand Dog Show! It's not quite like Crufts, ha, ha – we do things a bit differently down here – and in our Show there has been only one class, for The Most Lovable Dog. And the winner is . . . Ernest, the Gloucestershire Cowdog!'

And Sally gave Ernest a big hug, and the judge gave Sally a little cup, and the English Setter wagged his plumy tail like mad, and everybody clapped like billy-o,

and Ernest barked and barked so loudly
that he must have been heard by nearly
every cow in Gloucestershire.

Oh, the excitement of being Ernest!

# Norty Boy

Hylda was an old-fashioned sort of animal. She did not hold with the free and easy ways of the modern hedgehog, and even preferred to call herself by the old name of 'hedgepig'. She planned to bring up her seven hedgepiglets very strictly.

'Children should be seen and not heard' was one of her favourite sayings, and 'Speak when you're spoken to' was another. She taught them to say 'Please' and 'Thank you', to eat nicely, to sniff quietly if their noses were running, and never to scratch in public, no matter how many fleas they had.

Six of them – three boys and three girls – grew up to be well behaved, with beautiful manners, but the seventh was a great worry to Hylda and her husband Herbert. This seventh hedgepiglet was indeed the despair of Hylda's life. He was not only seen but constantly heard, speaking whether he was spoken to or not, and he never said 'Please' or 'Thank you'. He gobbled his food in a revolting slobbery way, he sniffed very loudly indeed, and he was forever scratching.

His real name was Norton, but he was more often known as Norty.

Now some mother animals can wallop their young ones if they do not do what they are told. A lioness can cuff her cub, a monkey can clip its child round the ear, or an elephant can give her baby a biff with her trunk. But it's not so easy for hedgehogs.

'Sometimes,' said Hylda to Herbert, 'I wish that hedgepigs didn't have prickles.'

'Why is that, my dear?' said Herbert.

'Because then I could give our Norty a good hiding. He deserves it.'

'Why is that, my dear?' said Herbert.

'Not only is he disobedient, he has taken to answering me back. Why can't he be good like the others? Never have I known such a hedgepiglet. I shall be glad when November comes.'

'Why is that, my dear?' said Herbert.

Hylda sighed. Conversation with my husband, she said to herself for the umpteenth time, can hardly be called interesting.

'Because then it's time to hibernate, of course, and we can all have a good sleep. For five blissful months I shall not have to listen to that impudent, squeaky, little voice arguing, complaining, refusing to do what I say and generally giving me cheek.'

Hylda should have known it would not be that easy.

When November came, she said to her husband and the seven children, 'Come along, all of you.'

'Yes, Mummy,' said the three good boys and the three good girls, and, 'Why is that, my dear?' said Herbert, but Norty only said, 'Shan't.'

'Norty,' said Hylda. 'If you do not do

what you are told, I shall get your father
to give you a good hard smack.'

Norty fluffed up his spines and sniggered.

'You'll be sorry if you do, Dad,' he said.

'Where are we going, Mummy?' asked
one of the hedgepiglets.

'We are going to find a nice deep bed
of dry leaves, where we can hibernate.'

'What does "hibernate" mean,
Mummy?' asked another.

'It means to go to sleep, all through

the winter. When it's rainy and blowy and frosty and snowy outside, we shall all be fast asleep under the leaf pile, all cosy and warm. Won't that be lovely?'

'No,' said Norty.

'Norton!' said his mother angrily. 'Are you coming or are you not?'

'No,' said Norty.

'Oh well, stay here then,' snapped Hylda, 'and freeze to death!' and she trotted off with the rest.

In a far corner of the garden they found a nice deep bed of dry leaves, and Hylda and Herbert and the six good hedgepiglets burrowed their way into it, and curled up tight, and shut their eyes, and went to sleep.

The following April they woke up, and opened their eyes, and uncurled, and burrowed out into the spring sunshine.

'Goodbye, Mummy. Goodbye, Daddy,' chorused the six good hedgepiglets, and off they trotted to seek their fortunes.

'Oh, Herbert,' said Hylda. 'I feel so sad.'

'Why is that, my dear?' said Herbert.

'I should never have left our Norty out in the cold last November. He will have frozen to death, poor little fellow. What does it matter that he was rude and disobedient and cheeky? Oh, if only I could hear his squeaky voice again, I'd be the happiest hedgepig ever!'

At that moment there was a rustling from the other side of the bed of leaves, and out came Norty.

'Can't you keep your voices down?' he said, yawning. 'A fellow can't get a wink of sleep.'

'Norty!' cried Hylda. 'You did hibernate, after all!'

'Course I did,' said Norty. 'What did you expect me to do – freeze to death?'

'Oh, my Norty boy!' said Hylda. 'Are you all right?'

'I was,' said Norty, 'till you woke me, nattering on as usual.'

'Now, now,' said Hylda, controlling herself with difficulty, 'that's not the way to speak to your mother, is it? Come here and give me a kiss.'

'Don't want to,' said Norty.

'Anyone would think,' said Hylda, 'that you weren't pleased to see us.'

'Anyone,' said Norty, 'would be right.'

'Well, push off then!' shouted Hylda. 'Your brothers and sisters have all gone, so get lost!'

'Shan't,' said Norty.

He yawned again, full in his mother's face.

'I'm going back to bed,' he said. 'So there.'

At this Hylda completely lost her temper.

'I've had enough!' she screamed. 'You're the rudest hedgepig in the world and your father's the most boring, and I never want to see either of you again!' and she ran away as fast as she could go.

Herbert and Norty stared after her.

Norty scratched his fleas and sniffed very noisily.

'Looks like she's done a bunk, Dad,' he said.

'Yes,' said Herbert. 'Why is that, my dear?'

'Can't think,' said Norty. 'But then she always was prickly.'

# The Clockwork Mouse

It really looked very much like a mouse.

Its round ears, its beady black eyes, its whiskers, its long thin tail, and especially its coat of greyish-brown hair were all so life-like. You would have thought it was a real live mouse, until you saw the round hole in its left side. That was the keyhole, and when you wound the mouse up with the little brass key, it scuttled across the room.

Jimmy had been given it for his seventh birthday, and at first he'd had a lot of fun with his clockwork mouse.

He'd frightened the life out of his big sister without even winding it up – he'd just put it quietly on her pillow so that when she woke, she was staring straight at it.

He'd let it run across the carpet just as his mother came into the sitting-room,

and she'd taken a huge jump right into an armchair.

And as for a bossy lady who came to tea and wouldn't stop talking, when the mouse ran straight at her feet, she stopped quick enough and started screaming instead, besides spilling hot tea in her lap, which made her hop about like a jumping jack.

Even the cat was fooled at first and

was about to pounce upon the clockwork mouse, so life-like was it.

But as time passed, everyone became used to Jimmy's toy, and he became bored with it, and, anyway, he lost the key.

So for many years now the clockwork mouse had lain at the bottom of the toy cupboard, gathering dust, until one day Jimmy's mother decided to have a clear-out and get rid of all the children's old toys.

She was packing them into a big cardboard box to take to Oxfam – dolls and model cars and jigsaws and board games and bits of Lego – when she came across the clockwork mouse. For a split second she thought it was a real one as it stared at her with its beady black eyes, and she went cold with sudden fright. But then she recognized it, and picked it up by its tail, holding it rather gingerly between her finger and thumb for the tail felt horribly real.

No key, she thought, Jimmy must have

lost it, so the thing's no use to anyone, and she dropped it into the waste-paper basket.

In due course the basket was emptied into the dustbin, and later the bin men came and tipped the contents of the dustbin into the refuse lorry. Possibly because it was small, the clockwork mouse escaped being squashed by the crusher inside the lorry, and so ended up all in one piece on the rubbish dump.

It rained that afternoon and washed all the dust and dirt off the toy, so that by nightfall it looked as good as new. Once again it looked life-like. So much so that later that night a scavenging fox, searching the dump for food scraps, picked it up in its jaws and carried it off.

At the edge of the field in which the rubbish was being dumped was a wood. In amongst the trees went the fox, mouse in mouth, and then dropped it on the ground. It was a young fox, not much more than a cub, but old enough to realize that this thing that looked like a mouse did not smell or feel like one, so it played with it for a while, tossing it up in the air, and then left it and padded off.

Hours later a little woodmouse, scuttling along through the leaf litter, came suddenly face to face with the toy. Coyly she touched noses with this handsome

stranger, but then her mate appeared and rushed angrily at the clockwork mouse, bowling it over and biting furiously at it.

At that moment the quavering, eerie call of a tawny owl rang out, and the woodmice vanished. Seconds later the owl came swooping low on silent wings and, seeing a motionless mouse, snatched it up and flew off with it. The three hungry owlets waiting in their nest in a hollow tree opened their beaks wide as they saw their mother approach, carrying food, but then they hissed angrily when they found they could not eat the strange, hard object she had brought, so she tossed it out of the nest-hole and flew off again.

The clockwork mouse lay at the foot of the hollow tree for months, until autumn came and the leaves fell and hid it from sight, forgotten by all the world. Only once was it remembered and that was because Jimmy's mother decided to have the old carpet in his bedroom replaced, and the carpet fitter found something wedged in a crack in the floor-boards.

'D'you know what this fits, Jimmy?' his mother said to him later, handing him a little brass key.

Jimmy looked at it and shook his head. But then he said, 'Wait a minute though. I remember now. It's the key to my clockwork mouse. Where is it, Mum?'

'I chucked it away, years and years ago.'

'Mum! It was my mouse!'

'Honestly, Jimmy,' his mother said, 'anyone would think you were still seven, instead of twice that age.'

'I liked that mouse,' Jimmy said. 'I shall keep the key anyway, in memory of the poor old chap.'

In fact, the poor old chap was on the move again.

A grey squirrel, searching through the bed of leaves on the floor of the wood, trying to remember where it had buried an acorn, had come upon the clockwork mouse and scratched at it angrily, kicking

it out into the open.

In the days that followed, a number of other woodland creatures came upon the mouse.

A badger picked it up in its great jaws and carried it a little way and dropped it again.

A weasel worried at it for a moment before tossing it aside.

A hedgehog nibbled at its fur and

found it tasteless.

A green woodpecker tapped it on the head with its strong beak.

And finally a magpie, nosiest of birds, carried it up to its nest of sticks in the top of an ash tree. The magpie, who liked bright things, had been attracted by the gleam in the beady black eyes of the toy, and the clockwork mouse spent the rest of that year in the magpie's nest, along with three bottle-tops, some pieces of coloured glass and a Coca-Cola can.

During the last part of the winter there were some severe gales, and in one of them the ash blew down. For many more months the clockwork mouse lay patiently among the tangle of fallen branches, until one day men came with chain-saws to cut up the tree.

'Look!' said one to another as they worked amid the lop and top. 'Here's a big bird's nest still in one piece. All sorts of rubbish in it too, and what's this? A mouse!'

'A live one, d'you mean?' said the other man.

'I thought it was for a minute,' said the woodcutter. 'Ever so life-like it is. But no, it's a clockwork mouse, would you believe it? See, here's the keyhole in the left side of it. How in the world did it ever get here?' and he stuffed it in his pocket.

'I've ordered a load of logs,' said Jimmy's father next day as he left for work. 'They should be delivered this morning. Some chaps have been cutting up a tree that was blown down in the wood next to the field where the rubbish dump used to be: before they filled it in and landscaped it, remember?'

'I've got to go out,' Jimmy's mother said.

'I'll be here,' said Jimmy. 'I'm not going to school today. I'm revising. I'll see to the logs.'

Later, when the woodcutter had unloaded the logs, Jimmy held out the

money his father had left with him.

'Half a tick,' said the woodcutter. 'There'll be a bit of change out of that,' and he put his hand in his pocket and brought out some coins, and with them something else.

'Look at this,' he said, and he put the clockwork mouse down on the bed of the pick-up truck.

Jimmy looked.

'Where did you find that?' he said.

'You'll never believe this,' the wood-cutter said, 'but that was in a bird's nest, a nest that had been in the top of the ash tree we cut these logs from. It's a clock-work mouse, see? No good to me – I haven't got any kids. And it's no good to you. Got any little brothers?'

'No,' said Jimmy, 'but you can leave it with me if you like.'

The woodcutter laughed.

'OK,' he said, 'you're welcome to it. But it's no use without a key,' and he handed over the toy and drove off.

Jimmy stood holding the clockwork mouse.

'You couldn't be, not after all these

years, could you?' he said, and then he thought – there's only one way to prove it's my mouse.

He fetched the little brass key and put it into the hole in the left side. It fitted! But it wouldn't turn.

'You must be terribly rusty,' said Jimmy, and he fetched the oil can he used on his bicycle and squirted some into the keyhole.

'Now then,' he said. 'Let's see if there's life in the old mouse yet,' and he began to wind. The mechanism was very stiff, but the key turned, just, and at last it was fully wound.

Then Jimmy set his old clockwork mouse on the floor, and slowly, noisily, jerkily it began to move across the carpet.

The passage of time had indeed aged it a great deal. Wind and weather had turned its coat a dirty yellow colour and the hair on it was patchy. Also it had run the gauntlet of a good many animals: one ear was weasel-chewed, its body bore assorted toothmarks, an owlet had taken off part of its tail, and there was a dent in the top of its head where the woodpecker had pecked it.

When it came to a halt, Jimmy picked it up and looked into its beady black eyes.

'I bet you could tell a story,' he said. 'I wonder whatever happened to you.'

The clockwork mouse stared back impassively.

# The Happiest Woodlouse

Walter was a wimp. He was scared of his own shadow – always had been since he was tiny.

No matter that he was now a really big woodlouse, with fourteen strong legs and a fine coat of armour, Walter was still afraid of everything and anything. Spiders, black beetles, centipedes, earwigs – whatever kind of creature he met frightened the life out of him, so that he rolled himself into a ball and wouldn't unroll again for ages.

Even with other woodlice he was just the same. Every time he met one, he rolled up and stayed rolled up until the patter of fourteen feet had died away in the distance.

You can easily understand why Walter had no friends.

I would like to make a friend, he said to himself. I would like to be able to have a good chat with someone, crack a joke or two perhaps. It must be nice to have a pal. If only I wasn't so nervous.

At that moment he heard someone approaching the large flat stone under which he was sheltering, and hastily he curled himself into a ball. The footsteps came nearer, and suddenly, to his horror, Walter felt himself being nudged. It was the sort of hefty nudge, Walter thought, that some fierce creature might give a wretched woodlouse before picking it up and swallowing it whole.

But then he heard a voice. It was a jolly voice which did not sound fierce but friendly.

'Wakey! Wakey!' said the voice. 'What's a chap like you doing all curled up on a nice sunny day like this, eh?'

Could this be the friend I've been waiting for, thought Walter?

'What are you?' he said, in somewhat muffled tones, for it is hard to speak clearly when you are curled up in a ball.

'I'm a woodlouse of course, like you,' said the voice. 'Come on, unroll, why don't you? Anyone would think you were afraid of something.'

If you only knew, said Walter to himself, I'm afraid of everything, but all the same he unrolled, to find himself face to face with a woodlouse of about his own size, but of a slightly different colour. Walter was slaty-grey. This stranger was paler, sort of brownish in fact, and freckled all over.

Walter waved his antennae.

'Hello,' he said. 'I'm Walter.'

'Hi,' said the stranger, waving back.

He looks a decent sort of chap, thought Walter. Well, it's now or never, so he took a deep breath and said, 'Will you be my friend?'

'My!' said the freckly stranger. 'You're a fast worker!'

'How do you mean?' said Walter.

'You don't waste time, do you? No remarks about the weather, no polite chit-chat, just "Will you be my friend?" Fair takes a girl's breath away!'

A girl, thought Walter! I just wanted a pal to have a chat with and crack a joke, but a girlfriend! Oh no, I'm frightened of girls. He was just about to curl up again when the stranger said, 'OK.'

Walter hesitated.

'OK what?' he said.

'OK, I'll be your friend, Walter. I've seen worse-looking woodlice than you. By the way, my name's Marilyn.'

'Oh,' said Walter.

He wiggled several pairs of legs
nervously.

'I'm pleased to meet you,' he said.

'You're a funny boy,' said Marilyn with a light laugh, and she moved forward until her antennae brushed gently against his.

At this touch something like an electric shock ran through every plate of Walter's armour and he found himself suddenly very short of breath.

'Come on,' said Marilyn. 'Let's go for a stroll.'

Ordinarily Walter never came out from beneath his large flat stone till nightfall. Spiders and black beetles and centipedes and earwigs were frightening enough, but in daylight, out in the open, there was far worse danger. Birds! Birds with sharp eyes and sharper beaks that snapped up spiders and black beetles and centipedes and earwigs – and woodlice!

'Can't we wait till after dark, Marilyn?' he said.

Marilyn giggled.

'Oh, you are a one!' she said, and out she went and off along the garden path.

Despite himself, Walter followed. He

was frightened, terrified indeed, but he hurried after Marilyn as fast as his seven pairs of legs could carry him. How beautiful she was, he now could see. Her long antennae, the slender legs, each delicate joint of her freckled carapace – all were perfection. Here, in the wide open spaces of the garden, death might threaten, but without Marilyn, thought Walter, life would not be worth living.

'Wait for me!' he called, but even as he spoke he saw to his horror that in the middle of the path ahead there squatted a huge slimy monster.

'Marilyn!' he cried. 'Watch out!' and hastily he rolled himself into a ball. Miserably he waited, tightly curled. Cruel Fate, thought Walter. I meet the love of my life and within minutes she walks down a monster's throat. If only I were brave, I might have tackled the brute. But I'm not, alas, I'm not.

Then a voice said, 'Are you coming, Walter, or aren't you?'

'What were you playing at?' said Marilyn when, sheepishly, he caught up with her. Of the monster there was no sign but a trail of slime across the flagstones.

Walter gulped.

'I thought I saw a monster,' he said.

'Monster?' said Marilyn. 'That was only an old slug. Mind where you're putting your feet, the path's all sticky.'

They walked on, off the path and on to a rose-bed under whose bushes was a scattering of dead leaves. On these they began to browse, side by side.

'Walter,' said Marilyn.

'Yes, Marilyn?'

'You've got a yellow streak, haven't you?'

Walter did not answer.

'Not to mince words,' said Marilyn, 'you're a chicken-hearted scaredy-cat and a cowardy-custard, aren't you?'

'Yes,' said Walter.

'Well, at least you've been honest with me,' said Marilyn, 'so I'll do the same for

you. Let's just forget the friendship bit.
You're a nice boy, but if there's one
thing I can't stand, it's a wimp. No hard
feelings, eh?'

'But, Marilyn . . .' said Walter.

'Yes?'

'I . . . I love you.'

For a moment Marilyn gazed thoughtfully at Walter. Such a good-looking fellow, but no backbone. Shame, really.

'Sorry, Walter,' she said. 'See you around, maybe,' and she turned to go.

As she did so, Walter saw the thrush come hopping through the rose-bed, straight towards her.

Even as he tensed his muscles to roll himself into a ball, something snapped in his brain, and instead he rushed forward on his fourteen powerful legs.

'Roll up, quick!' he shouted at Marilyn, shoving her out of his way, and then, as instinctively she obeyed, Walter made directly for the huge bird.

'Take me!' he cried. 'Take me, you brute, but spare my Marilyn!'

The thrush put its head on one side,

the better to focus upon this foolhardy woodlouse, when it saw from the corner of its other eye a fat worm. Leaving Walter for afters, it picked up the worm and swallowed it.

As it was doing so, a large tabby cat came strolling down the garden path, waving its tail, and the thrush flew hastily away.

'All clear!' cried Walter, and Marilyn unrolled.

'You saved my life!' she breathed.

'Well, I don't know about that,' said Walter in an embarrassed voice.

'Well, you jolly well tried to,' said Marilyn. 'You were ready to sacrifice yourself to protect me, weren't you?'

'Yes,' said Walter.

Marilyn stared at her gallant knight in armour.

To think, she said to herself, that I called him a cowardy-custard. Her heart swelled within her bosom, and she went weak at the knees, all fourteen of them.

'Oh Walter,' she said softly, 'I am yours, all yours.'

'Oh Marilyn,' said Walter. 'You have made me the happiest woodlouse in the world!'

# Use Your Brains

Little Basil Brontosaurus came home from his first morning at playschool in floods of tears.

'Whatever's the matter, darling?' said his mother, whose name was Araminta. 'Why are you crying?'

'They've been teasing me,' sobbed Basil.

'Who have? The other children?'

A variety of little dinosaurs went to

the playschool. There were diplodocuses, iguanodons, ankylosauruses and many others. Basil was the only young brontosaurus.

'Yes,' sniffed Basil. 'They said I was stupid. They said I hadn't got a brain in my head.'

At this point Basil's father, a forty-ton brontosaurus who measured eighty feet from nose to tail-tip, came lumbering up through the shallows of the lake in which the family lived.

'Herb!' called Araminta. 'Did you hear that? The kids at playschool said our Basil hadn't a brain in his head.'

Herb considered this while pulling up and swallowing large quantities of water-weed.

'He has,' he said at last. 'Hasn't he?'

'Of course you have, darling,' said Araminta to her little son. 'Come along with me now, and dry your tears and listen carefully.'

Still snivelling, Basil waded into the

lake and followed his mother to a secluded inlet, well away from the other dinosaurs that were feeding around the shallows.

Araminta settled herself where the water was deep enough to help support her enormous bulk.

'Now listen to Mummy, Basil darling,' she said. 'What I'm about to tell you is a secret. Every brontosaurus that ever hatched is told this secret by his or her mummy or daddy, once he or she is old enough. One day you'll be grown up, and you'll have a wife of your own, and she'll lay eggs, and then you'll have babies. And when those babies are old enough, they'll have to be told, just like I'm going to tell you.'

'Tell me what?' said Basil.

'Promise not to breathe a word of it to the other children?'

'All right. But what is it?'

'It is this,' said Araminta. 'We have two brains.'

'You're joking,' said Basil.

'I'm not. Every brontosaurus has two brains. One in its head and one in the middle of its back.'

'Wow!' cried Basil. 'Well, if I've got two brains and all the other kids have only got one, I must be twice as clever as them.'

'You are, darling,' said Araminta. 'You are. So let's have no more of this cry-baby nonsense. Next time one of the children teases you, just think to yourself "I am twice as clever as you".'

Not only did Basil think this, next morning at playschool, but he also thought that he was twice as big as the other children.

'Did you have a nice time?' said Araminta, when he came home.

'Smashing,' said Basil.

'No tears?'

'Not mine,' said Basil cheerily.

'You didn't tell anyone our secret?'

'Oh no,' said Basil. 'I didn't do much talking to the other kids. Actions speak louder than words.'

Not long after this the playschool teacher, an elderly female stegosaurus, came to see Herb and Araminta.

'I'm sorry to bother you,' she said, 'but I'm a little worried about Basil.'

'Not been blubbing again, has he?' said Herb.

'Oh no, *he* hasn't,' said the stegosaurus. 'In fact, recently he has grown greatly in confidence. At first he was rather nervous and the other children tended to make fun of him, but they don't any more. Something seems to have given him a great deal of self-assurance. He's twice the boy he was.'

'Can't think why,' said Herb, but Araminta could.

'Indeed,' went on the stegosaurus, 'I fear that lately he's been throwing his weight about. Boys will be boys, I know, but really Basil has become very rough. Only yesterday I had to send home a baby brachiosaurus with a badly bruised foot and a little trachodon with a black eye. I should be glad if you would speak to Basil about all this.'

When the teacher had departed, Araminta said to Herb, 'You must have a word with the boy.'

'Why?' said Herb.

'You heard what the teacher said. He's been bullying the other children. He's obviously getting above himself.'

At this point Basil appeared.

'What did old Steggy want?' he said.

'Tell him, Herb,' said Araminta.

'Now look here, my boy,' said Herb.

Basil looked.

'You listen to me.'

Basil listened, but Herb, Araminta could see, had lost the thread of the matter.

'Your father is very angry with you,' she said. 'You have been fighting. At play-school.'

'That's right,' said Herb. 'Fighting. At playschool. Why?'

'Well, it's like this, Dad,' said Basil. 'The first day, the other kids teased me. They said I hadn't got a brain in my head, remember? And then Mum told me I had. And another in the middle of my back. Two brains! So I thought I'm twice as clever as the rest as well as twice as big, so why not lean on them a bit? Not my fault if they get under my feet.'

'You want to watch your step,' said Herb.

'Daddy's right,' said Araminta. 'One of these days you'll get into real trouble. Now run along, I want to talk to your father.'

'It's all my fault for telling him about having two brains,' she said when Basil had gone. 'He's too young. My parents didn't tell me till I was nearly grown-up. How did you find out?'

'Oh, I don't know,' said Herb. 'I dare say I heard some of the chaps talking.

Down in the swamp. When I was one of the gang. We used to talk a lot, down in the swamp.'

'What about?' said Araminta.

'Water-weed, mostly,' said Herb, and he pulled up a great mouthful and began to chomp.

Not long after this, Basil was expelled.

'I'm sorry,' said the elderly stegosaurus, 'but I can't have the boy in my class any longer. It isn't only his roughness, it's his rudeness. Do you know what he said to me today?'

'No,' said Herb.

'What?' said Araminta.

'He said to me "I'm twice as clever as you are".'

'Is he?' said Herb.

'Of course he isn't,' said Araminta hastily. 'He was just being silly and childish. I'm sure he won't be any trouble in the future.'

'Not in my playschool he won't,' said

the stegosaurus and then, oddly, she used the very words that Araminta had used earlier.

'One of these days,' she said, 'he'll get into real trouble,' and off she waddled, flapping her plates angrily.

And one of those days, Basil did.

Being expelled from playschool hadn't worried him at all. What do I want with other dinosaurs, he thought. I'm far superior to them, with my two brains, one to work my neck and my front legs, one to work my back legs and my tail. Brontosauruses are twice as clever as other dinosaurs and I'm twice as clever as any other brontosaurus.

You couldn't say that Basil was bigheaded for that was almost the smallest part of him, but you could certainly say that he was boastful, conceited and arrogant.

'That boy!' said Araminta to Herb. 'He's boastful, conceited and arrogant.

He must get it from your side of the family, swaggering about and picking fights all the time. What does he think he is? A tyrannosaurus rex?'

'What do you think you are?' Basil was saying at that very moment. He had come out of the lake where the family spent almost all their time, and set off for a walk.

He was ambling along, thinking what a fine fellow he was, when he suddenly saw a strange, smallish dinosaur standing in his path.

It was not like any dinosaur he had ever seen before. It stood upright on its hind legs which were much bigger than its little forelegs, and it had a large head with large jaws and a great many teeth. But compared to Basil, who already weighed a couple of tons, it looked quite small, and he advanced upon it, saying in a rude tone, 'What do you think you are?'

'I'm a tyrannosaurus rex,' said the stranger.

'Never heard of you,' said Basil.

'Lucky you.'

'Why? What's so wonderful about you? You can't even walk on four feet like a decent dinosaur and you've only got one brain. You'll be telling me next that you don't eat water-weed like we do.'

'We don't,' said the other. 'We only eat meat.'

'What sort of meat?'

'Brontosaurus, mostly.'

'Let's get this straight,' said Basil. 'Are you seriously telling me that you kill brontosauruses and eat them?'

'Yes.'

'Don't make me laugh,' said Basil. 'I'm four times as big as you.'

'Yes,' said the youngster, 'but my dad's four times as big as you. Oh look, what a bit of luck, here he comes!'

Basil looked up to see a terrifying sight.

Marching towards him on its huge

hind legs was a towering, full-grown tyrannosaurus rex. In its forepaws it held the remains of the body of some wretched smaller dinosaur, from which it tore mouthfuls with its battery of six-inch teeth. Blood dripped from its mighty jaws as it chewed and swallowed, and all of a sudden Basil had two brainwaves.

Time I went, he thought. Sharpish. And as one brain sent a message rippling along to the other, he turned tail and made for the safety of the lake as fast as his legs could carry him.

Like all his kind, he was slow and clumsy on land, and if his pursuer had not recently made a kill, Basil must surely have been its next victim.

As it was, he reached the shore of the lake in time and splashed frantically out to deeper water, where his parents, their long necks downstretched, were browsing on the weedy bottom.

Araminta was the first to look up.

'Hello, darling,' she said. 'Where have

you been? Whatever's the matter? You're all of a doodah.'

'Oh Mummy, Mummy!' panted Basil. 'It was awful! I went for a walk and I was nearly eaten by a tyrannosaurus rex!'

Herb raised his head in time to hear this.

'That'll teach you,' he said.

'Teach me what, Dad?'

'Not to be so cocky,' said Araminta.

'Ever since I told you that secret you've been unbearable, Basil. I hope this will be a lesson to you.'

'Oh, it will, Mummy, it will!' cried Basil. 'I won't ever shoot my mouth off again.'

'And don't go for walks,' said his mother, 'but keep close to the lake where you'll be safe from the tyrannosaurus.'

'In case he rex you,' said Herb and plunged his head underwater again, while strings of bubbles rose as he laughed at his own joke.

'And if you want to grow up to be as big as your father,' said Araminta, 'there's one thing you must always remember to do.'

'What's that, Mummy?' said Basil.

'Use your brains.'

# Philibert the
# First and
# Other Stories

# Contents

Philibert the First      113

George Starts School      126

Carol Singing      143

Maisie Grazer      164

Banger      180

Poor Edgar      187

# Philibert the First

Felicia was a wonderful country.

Every Monday was a Bank Holiday and no one worked on a day with an S in it (which just left Friday).

It never rained in the daytime but only at night.

There were no traffic problems because everyone rode about (very slowly) on donkeys.

And there were no schools. If you wanted to know something, you asked your mum or dad, and if they didn't know how many beans make five, then neither would you.

Finally, even if they didn't always actually love their neighbours, Felicians were always nice to one another, so that everyone was happy. Except the King.

King Philibert the First of Felicia had everything anyone could want. He had his health and strength, he had a beautiful wife and three handsome sons and three pretty daughters, and a magnificent palace and loads of servants and pots of money and a pet walrus called Norman. What more could any man desire?

Yet King Philibert had become unhappy and not a single Felician knew the reason why, not even the Queen.

'Philibert,' she would say each day. 'Why are you unhappy?' And each day the King would reply, 'I'm sorry, my dear, but I do not know.'

"You do still love me, don't you?" the Queen would say, and the King would answer "Yes, my dear, I do," but oh, how sadly he said it.

It was the same with the little princes and princesses. On Fridays those that could read studied the *Encyclopaedia Felicianica* and those that could only weed worked in the Palace gardens. But on every other day they too asked their father, 'Why are you unhappy, Papa?' and the King would reply, 'I'm sorry, my children, I wish I knew why.'

Everyone else wished so too,

because all of them, right down to the poorest beggar in the streets of the capital, FeliCity, were as happy as larks, while their King was as miserable as sin, with a face as long as a boot.

Only one living creature in Felicia looked as sad as King Philibert, and that was his pet walrus, Norman.

Norman was twelve feet long and so fat that he weighed a ton and a half. Some Felicians on an expedition to Greenland had brought him back as a fiftieth birthday present for the King.

Norman's favourite food was oysters, and every morning King Philibert would feed him dozens of them (except when there was an R in the month, and then Norman had to make do with mussels).

And every morning the King would pat the walrus on top of his huge round bald head, and say sadly, 'There, was that nice?' and in reply Norman would give a deep gurgly moan that sounded like 'Gloom!' Then the King and his pet walrus would stare sorrowfully at one another, the very picture of unhappiness.

'I never can decide,' said the Queen to the little princes and princesses, 'which looks the more miserable.'

She had of course often consulted the Royal Doctor about the King's condition, but though he had suggested dieting, and exercise, and hot and cold baths, and even taking the day off on Fridays, nothing had worked. Even the Court Jester's funniest jokes could raise no smile on the face of King Philibert the First of Felicia.

One morning as the King finished feeding his walrus with oysters, he said with a sigh, 'Very soon, Norman, I shall be fifty-one, and then it will be a whole year since first you arrived and since last I smiled.'

'Gloom!' answered Norman.

And gloom there was, a day or so later, for the walrus was suddenly taken ill with the stomach-ache. To the one usual word he spoke was added another.

'Doom!' moaned Norman. 'Doom!'

Feeling sadder than ever, the King sent for the Royal Vet.

Now it so happened that the Royal Vet was newly appointed and had never before set eyes on King Philibert, let alone on Norman.

'What seems to be the trouble, Your Majesty?' he asked politely.

'It's Norman,' said the King sadly. 'He has the tummy-ache, poor fellow. This morning he actually refused his food.'

'What food, Sire?' asked the Royal Vet.

'Oysters, of course.'

'In the second week of May?' said the Royal Vet.

'Oh help!' said King Philibert. 'I was thinking it was still April. There's no R in this month.'

'Exactly,' said the Royal Vet. 'No wonder he has the tummy-ache.'

'Doom!' groaned Norman.

'We'll soon put him right,' said the Royal Vet. 'Starve him for a couple of days and then switch to mussels and

he'll be as right as rain.'

The King sighed.

The Royal Vet looked carefully at his royal master.

'Forgive me, Sire,' he said, 'if I say that you do not look as happy as the average Felician. In fact you do not look at all happy. In fact you look downright wretched.'

'I am,' said King Philibert. 'Soon it will be a year since last I smiled.'

The Royal Vet looked extremely thoughtful.

'How long, may I ask,' he said, 'has Your Majesty kept this walrus as a pet?'

'Almost a year,' said the King. 'He was a fiftieth birthday present and soon I shall be fifty-one.'

'That's it!' cried the Royal Vet.

'That's what?' cried the King.

'Gloom!' moaned the walrus.

'Norman,' said the Royal Vet, 'is the cause of Your Majesty's unhappiness. Looking at Norman's gloomy face has made you gloomy too.'

'Must I get rid of him then?' said the King. 'Must Norman go?'

'No, no, Sire,' said the Royal Vet. 'What we must do is to turn Norman into a happy walrus, and I think I know how to do this.'

'How?' asked the King.

'Leave it to me, Your Majesty,' said the Royal Vet.

So King Philibert left it to him.

Thus it was that, some months later, another expedition arrived back from Greenland with another present for the King.

It was another walrus, much like Norman to look at, but smaller. When he saw it, King Philibert looked even sadder than usual.

'If one walrus makes me miserable,' he said, 'what will two do?'

But Norman didn't look sadder than usual. Norman didn't look as sad as usual. Norman didn't look sad at all.

His dull fishy eyes suddenly lit up at the sight of the new walrus, his moustache bristled, his mournful expression turned into a kind of a grin. Then he opened his mouth and out of it came, not the usual 'Gloom!' or 'Doom!' but a happy excited roaring noise that sounded like 'Vroom! Vroom!' as he lumbered forward to touch noses with the newcomer.

'He likes him,' said King Philibert.

'He likes her, you mean,' said the Royal Vet.

'Oh,' said the King. 'I see. You mean . . .?'

'I mean, Your Majesty,' said the Royal Vet, 'that from now on Norman will be a different animal. Just look at him!'

And King Philibert looked at his happy walrus, and a great smile spread over his face. Then he began to chuckle, and then he began to laugh, so loudly that the Queen and the three little princes and the three little princesses and all the members of the

Royal Household came running to see what on earth had happened.

Oh, what joy there was throughout the land of Felicia as the glad news of the King's recovery became known!

Happy as the people had thought themselves before, now they were even happier, especially when they learned that in celebration a Royal Decree had been issued, forbidding anyone to work on Fridays.

'Oh, Philibert!' said the Queen when at last they were alone together. 'You do still love me, don't you?'

'Yes, my dear,' said King Philibert the First of Felicia. 'I am very, very glad to say I do. Without the shadow of a doubt we shall live happily ever after.'

And they did.

# George Starts School

One morning, not long after George's fourth birthday, his mother was watching him as he sat at the breakfast table, reading the *Financial Times*. His father had just left for work, taking George's eleven-year-old sister Laura with him, to school.

'Just think, George,' said his mother. 'Only two more terms and then you'll be going to school too. You'll be a Rising-Five.'

'I am aware of my age, Mother,' said George, turning a page (with difficulty, for the newspaper was large), 'and sometimes I feel it.'

'You'll like school, won't you, George?' said his mother. George put down the *Financial Times* with a sigh.

'The answer to that question,' he said, 'can only be hypothetical. Whether I shall "like" school, as you put it, has yet to be proven. Judging by what I read of the new curriculum, I shall not.'

'Why, is it too difficult?'

'Too easy,' said George, and he picked up the newspaper once more.

It was his mother's turn to sigh, a sigh partly of resignation to the fact that George always had the last word, and partly of pride at her most unusual son. She sat drinking her coffee and remembering how fantastically early George had learned to speak, how fluent he was in the English language when less than six months old. Neither she nor her husband had ever known (because Laura had never

revealed it) that in fact George was holding long conversations with his sister a mere four weeks after his birth, when he knew a great deal more than she did, including his multiplication tables.

'It's a pity,' she said reflectively, 'that there's a seven-year gap between you and Laura. When you go to primary school, she'll have left.'

'Just as well,' said George.

'What do you mean? Don't you like your sister?'

'Mother,' said George patiently, 'I am in point of fact extremely fond of Laura, but I am perfectly accustomed to doing without her during the day. Things will be no different.'

'Yes, but when Laura's at school, I'm always with you, George. I shan't be then. You'll be all alone.'

'According to Laura,' said George, 'there are a hundred and fifty children at the school which I am to attend, not to mention all the teachers, the secretary, the dinner ladies, the caretaker and the odd-job man. I shall not be alone.'

His mother remembered these last words on the day, eight months later, when she walked, holding George by the hand, through the playground full of hordes of rushing yelling children. She looked down at her little son, so much smaller, it seemed, than nearly all the others, and saw that he was frowning.

'It's sure to be strange at first, George,' she said. 'But I'll be here to fetch you after school. Don't worry.'

'I am not worried, Mother,' said George. 'Merely appalled at the noise and general confusion. How childishly everyone is behaving.'

In Class 5, the reception class, the teacher, who was also new at the school and had never before set eyes on George or any of the other children, was filling in her register. Everyone had been shown a peg to hang their coats on, and a locker to keep their things in, and given a place to sit, and some crayons and paper to draw on. As each new child in turn was called to the teacher's desk, she wrote down their names in the register and, if they knew them, their dates of birth.

'Now then, who are you?' she asked when it was George's turn.

'My name,' said George, 'is George.'

'And do you know when your birthday is, George?'

"It is April the first," said George.

"April Fool's Day," said the teacher smiling.

George did not smile.

"You will find," he said severely, "that I am nobody's fool."

Later, the teacher went round looking at the pictures the children had drawn. Some were of their animals, some of their houses, some of their parents, and one little girl had actually written MUM under her picture.

'That's very good!' said the teacher.

Then she came to George.

If people's eyes could really pop out of their heads, George's new teacher would have gone blind at that instant, for George's picture,

1988 Honda Goldwing Aspencade.

minute in detail, was of a motorcycle. Under it was written in joined-up writing,

*1988 Honda Goldwing Aspencade.*

'George!' gasped the teacher. 'What in the world . . .?'

'I am interested in motorcycles,' said George, 'amongst other things. This is a Japanese tourer. It has a flat four 1182 c.c. engine, a 5-speed gearbox and transistorized ignition.'

George's second day at school was spent in Class 4, and by the end of the week he was in Class 1, among the ten- and eleven-year-olds. The children treated him with the awed respect they might have accorded to an

alien from outer space, and the teachers were, quite simply, flabbergasted.

The headmaster had at first paid little heed to rumours of George's abilities, but that Friday was one that he never forgot.

In the morning, he taught Class 1.

At lunch time, he summoned George to his study.

'Sit down, George,' he said in a kindly voice.

'I can't,' said George.

'Why not?'

'I fear the chair is too high for me,' said George, so the headmaster lifted him on to it.

'Now, George,' he said. 'I just want to ask you some questions. How old are you?'

'Four years and eleven months,' said George.

'They tell me you can do joined-up writing.'

'Up to a point,' said George. 'My physical skills are inferior to my mental abilities.'

'Ah,' said the headmaster in a shaky voice. 'What about numbers?'

'Mathematics, d'you mean?' said George. 'My knowledge is purely in the realm of arithmetic so far. Algebra and geometry are treats in store for me.'

'And reading?' croaked the head-master.

'Reading,' said George, 'is something I find most enjoyable. There are a great many excellent children's authors published these days, but I must confess to a weakness for the older classics. Take for example *Alice in Wonderland*. What a work of fantasy!'

'Fantastic!' whispered the head-master.

After lunch Class 1 was working on a project about South America, drawing maps and putting in the capital cities and principal rivers and mountain ranges. To be fair to the headmaster, he knew the names of the capitals of most of the countries of South America, but on one he momen-tarily stumbled.

'The capital of Guyana is . . .' he said. 'Silly of me, it's slipped my mind. Look it up, someone.'

'No need,' said a very young but already familiar voice. 'It's Georgetown.'

That evening George went to bed early.

'I'm quite tired,' he said to his parents

and Laura. 'It's been a busy week.'

'It's amazing,' said his father later. 'To be in the top class, his first week of school!'

'He's top of the top class!' said his mother.

'He's miles cleverer than me!' said Laura proudly. 'He won't need me for help with homework, I'll need him.' George's mother sighed. This time it was a deep sigh of pure regret.

'I just wish he needed me still,' she said. 'He never seems to, now.'

Just then there was an awful wailing from upstairs.

It was a terrified wailing, the cry of a very young child that desperately wants its mother.

'Mummy! Mummy! Mummy!' cried George from the darkness of his bedroom.

'I'm coming, my baby!' called George's mother. 'Mummy's coming!' and she rushed upstairs to find George sitting up in bed, sobbing his heart out. This was not the confident self-assured know-it-all cleverest child in the school. This was just a frightened baby, and she cuddled him as fiercely as she had when he was only tiny and had never spoken a word.

'What is it, George darling?' she said as she mopped away his tears. 'Did you have a bad dream?'

'I did, I did, Mummy!' sobbed George.

'What was it? Tell Mummy.'

Gradually George's sobs turned to sniffles, and then he blew his nose and said, 'I dreamt we were doing a science test at school.'

'A science test?'

'Yes, we do science in the new curriculum, you know. And there was a simple question in it that I couldn't answer, and I cried like a baby. I cried in the dream, and I was crying when I woke up. I really must apologize for behaving so childishly.'

'Poor lamb!' said his mother. 'What was the question?'

'It was the order of events in the cycle of the internal combustion engine,' said George.

'Forget about it, George,' said his mother sadly. 'I expect there'll be lots of questions you won't know the answers to.'

'Not if I can help it,' said George.

'Anyway, don't worry. Just go back to sleep. Mummy's here.'

'Oh, I shan't worry any more, Mother,' said George in his usual confident tones. 'I've remembered it now. It's Induction – Compression – Ignition – Exhaust,' and exhausted, he lay back and went happily to sleep.

# Carol Singing

Christmas was coming, and one of the teachers was banging away on the piano, as the school practised for the end-of-term service.

'O come, let us adore Him!' sang all one hundred and twenty children.

At any rate one hundred and nineteen of them sang, while the one hundred and twentieth opened her mouth and made a dreadful noise.

'Oh, that voice!' said the head-mistress afterwards, as she drank her coffee in the staffroom. 'You can hear it above all the rest.'

'It's like a cow mooing,' said someone.

'No, more like a pig squealing.'

'Or a dog howling.'

'And to think,' said the headmistress, 'that when that child was born, her parents chose to call her Carol!'

'It's pathetic really,' said Carol's class teacher. 'She loves singing.'

'Singing, you call it?'

'I mean, she loves music. She knows all the words, of all the carols, Carol does.'

'But not the tunes.'

'No, I'm afraid she has absolutely no ear for music.'

'Unfortunately,' said the headmistress, 'we each have two ears and Carol's frightful voice is all I can hear. No matter how nicely the other children sing "I saw three ships come sailing by", all I can hear is that foghorn bellowing its warning of rocks ahead. For goodness' sake, when it comes to the church service, try to get her to keep her voice down.'

'Why don't you keep your voice down?' a catty girl called Catherine was saying to Carol out in the playground.

'I didn't speak,' said Carol.

'I don't mean now. I mean when we're singing. You're awful, you are. You're tone-deaf.'

'What's that mean?' asked Carol.

'It means,' said a know-all girl called Noelle, 'that you can't tell differences in musical pitch. I've got perfect pitch, I have.'

'It sounds all right inside my head,' Carol said.

'Well, keep it in there,' they said. 'Don't let it out to give everyone else a headache.'

It had always been the same. It wasn't too bad when Carol first went to school, because quite a few of the infants weren't all that good at singing in tune. But as time passed and they all grew older, everyone else seemed to get the hang of it. Of course not all of the children had good voices, but they all seemed to rub along all right and those that weren't brilliant at least had the sense to sing softly.

But not Carol. She liked to keep going full blast, and if she ever hit a right note, it was a complete fluke.

The day of the carol service dawned, and Carol's teacher watched anxiously as the children came in through the classroom door. It's not nice of me, she thought, but if only Carol could have a cold today, the kind that makes you lose your voice. But there was no such luck.

'Sing a bit quietly today, Carol, won't you?' the teacher said before they set out.

'Why?'

'Well, you do . . . shout a bit.'

But even though the church was full of mums and dads and grandparents and many others as well as all the children, and even though her teacher had put Carol at the very far end of a pew and behind a large pillar, still she could clearly be heard through all the singing.

Some people were amused and smiled, some frowned angrily, several babies burst out crying, and one of the grandfathers switched off his hearing aid, as, through carol after carol, there sounded the drones and groans and moans of that awful voice.

'It isn't as if she was just a bit sharp or flat,' said know-all Noelle afterwards. 'She's just absolutely tuneless.'

'Oh, I don't know,' said catty Catherine. 'She wasn't too bad on the Amens,' and they went off together, giggling.

Carol walked home alone, wondering for the thousandth time why it was that, though she could hear the tunes clearly in her mind, they came out all wrong.

'I *wish* I could sing properly,' she said, and then she had an idea.

'Why shouldn't I be taught?' she said. 'After all, you can be taught anything – how to read, how to write, how to do sums, and later on things like how to drive a car. Why can't you be taught to sing?'

So as soon as she got home, she opened the Yellow Pages.

SINGING TUITION (she found) see MUSIC TEACHERS

There were several names under this heading, and one was in the very next street to hers. She went to find her mother.

'Mum,' she said. 'Can I have singing lessons?'

'Why?' said Carol's mother. What's the use, she thought.

'I just want to learn to sing in tune, that's all. I can hear the music in my head, but when I open my mouth, it comes out all funny.'

'I know, dear.'

'And look, there's a music teacher in the next street, Mum,' said Carol, and she pointed to the place in the Yellow Pages.

'Who's going to pay for these lessons?' asked her mother.

'Me. I'll save up. Honest. Can I have them? Please?'

'We'd better go and see,' said Carol's mother.

So next morning, a Saturday, they went together to a little house in the next street and knocked on the door. On it was a notice

MISS N. CHANTER
MUSIC TEACHER

It was opened by a little old lady with grey hair done in a bun and the nicest, smiliest sort of face.

'Hullo,' she said. 'What can I do for you?'

'My daughter wants singing lessons,' said Carol's mother. 'How much do you charge?'

'That depends,' said Miss N. Chanter. 'Come in, and we'll see.'

She led them into a small room
mostly filled by a large piano, on top
of which a black cat lay sleeping.

Miss N. Chanter sat down at the
piano.

'Now then,' she said, 'what's your
name?'

'Carol.'

'Hm. Do you like music?'

'Oh yes! I like all sorts of music
and I know loads of different tunes. I

can hear them all in my head perfectly, but when I open my mouth they don't come out quite right. I just want to be able to sing properly, like everyone else at school.'

'Well, let's try,' said Miss N. Chanter, and she played the first few bars of 'God save the Queen'.

'Know the words?' she said.

'Oh yes!'

'OK. Let's go. One . . . two . . .'

'Well, well,' said Miss N. Chanter after the last quavering 'Queen' had died away and the black cat had dashed from the room with all his fur standing on end, 'I see what you mean, Carol. Or rather I hear what you mean. We have problems.'

'You mean you can't teach me?' said Carol.

'I didn't say that.'

'You mean it's going to cost a lot of money?' said Carol's mother.

'I didn't say that either. In fact, if I can't teach Carol to sing, I won't charge you a penny.'

That's all right then, thought Carol's mother, she hasn't got a hope.

So they fixed that Carol should come by herself for her first lesson in a week's time.

'I've had an idea!' was the first thing Miss N. Chanter said when she opened the door to Carol on the next Saturday morning. 'I believe you when you say you can hear tunes in your head but it's what comes out of your mouth that's the trouble. Now, if we could catch the tunes on their way out . . .'

'I don't understand,' said Carol.

Miss N. Chanter put her hand in

the pocket of her woolly cardigan and
took out a small mouth-organ. She
held it out to Carol.

'Try this,' she said.

'But I can't play any instrument,'
said Carol.

'This isn't just any instrument. Try
playing a tune on it. Low notes on the
left, high notes on the right. All you've
got to do is blow and suck. Go on.'

Carol hesitated. This is silly, she

thought, I've never played a mouth-organ before. It will just be a horrid noise, and, as though she had spoken out loud, Miss N. Chanter said, 'No, it won't. Choose something simple, a nursery rhyme, say. How about "Pop Goes the Weasel", know the tune of that? Right then, just sing it in your head and suck and blow.'

Just what it was that made her move the mouth-organ to left or to right or told her when to suck and when to blow Carol never could after-wards understand. But she never forgot the playing of that first simple little tune. Every note was right. No one could have played "Pop Goes the Weasel" better. Even the black cat purred loudly.

'I thought as much,' said Miss N. Chanter. 'It's just a question of catching the melody that's in your head before it gets out into the open air. Now choose another tune.'

So Carol chose 'Widecombe Fair' and the tune came out perfectly, every bit of it, old Uncle Tom Cobley and all!

Carol took the mouth-organ out of her mouth and stared at it in wonder.

'It's magic!' she said.

'You could say that,' said Miss N. Chanter.

'It's wonderful,' said Carol, 'but . . .'

'But what?'

'. . . but how will it teach me to sing?'

Miss N. Chanter sat down at the piano and played the scale of C Major.

Then with one finger she struck middle C.

'Play that,' she said.

Carol played it.

'Now this time,' said Miss N. Chanter, 'I'll hit the note again, you play it, and then quickly take the thing out of your mouth and sing it – "Lah".'

And it worked! Carol sang the perfect middle C!

After that it was plain sailing.

At the second lesson Carol could

play a scale on the mouth-organ and then she was managing without the mouth-organ, singing to Miss N. Chanter's accompaniment on the piano, and by the end of the tenth lesson she could sing any tune unaccompanied.

'That's it, then, Carol,' said Miss N. Chanter. 'You can sing. And what's more, you've a very good voice.'

'It's all thanks to you and your mouth-organ,' said Carol. 'Please, how much do I owe you?'

'Oh, we'll see about that,' said Miss N. Chanter. 'Now let's have one last song. How about "Over the Rainbow"? D'you know that?'

'Oh yes!' cried Carol. 'How funny you should choose that! We're going to do *The Wizard of Oz* for the school concert this term.'

'Fancy!' said Miss N. Chanter. 'Tell you what, Carol. If you get the part of Dorothy, I won't charge you a penny.'

'Who's going to play Dorothy?' said the headmistress to the teacher who was organizing the concert.

'Oh, Noelle, I should think,' said the teacher. 'She's got perfect pitch and not a bad voice. There are a number of girls who might be good enough. I'll have an audition.'

'Don't bother with Carol,' the headmistress said, and everybody laughed.

You can guess the rest, can't you?

Half a dozen girls tried for the part of Dorothy, and know-all Noelle was maybe the best. But before she could be told so, one more girl had come into the room.

'What are you doing here, Carol?' the teacher said. 'We're auditioning for *The Wizard of Oz*, you know.'

'She could make the noises for the Cowardly Lion,' said catty Catherine, and the others sniggered.

'Please,' said Carol. 'I want to be Dorothy.'

'Carol must have the part beyond the shadow of a doubt,' said the teacher to the headmistress afterwards. 'She put me in mind of the young Judy Garland. She sang "Over the Rainbow" quite beautifully. She'll bring the house down!'

'I cannot understand it,' said the headmistress. 'It smacks of witch-craft.'

And you won't be surprised to hear that, at the end of the school concert, among the clapping, cheering audience that stood to applaud the wonderful singing of Carol as Dorothy in *The Wizard of Oz* was a little old lady with grey hair done in a bun and the nicest, smiliest sort of face.

# Maisie Grazer

You don't expect a name to *mean* anything, do you?

Someone called Baker doesn't necessarily grow up to make bread, nor does a Barber have to cut hair, and if your name is Smellie, it doesn't mean you are.

So no one thought there was anything odd when a Mr Grazer married a Miss Meadows.

After a while Mrs Grazer had a baby, a little girl, and they called her Maisie.

A very normal baby was Maisie Grazer, or so it seemed at first. It was not till Maisie's mother started her on solid foods that the Grazers noticed anything strange.

'It's funny,' said Mrs Grazer to her husband. 'Maisie doesn't seem to like the usual baby foods – liver-and-bacon, minced beef, lamb casserole, that sort of thing. She won't eat any of them.'

'Maybe she doesn't like the meat in them,' said Mr Grazer. 'Perhaps she's going to be a vegetarian.'

'You're joking,' said Mrs Grazer, but all the same she bought some Purée of Spinach, and Maisie gollopped it down. In fact she seemed to like it so much that she spoke her first word.

'Moo,' she said.

'Did you hear that?' cried Mrs Grazer. 'She said "More"!'

'It sounded like "Moo" to me,' said Mr Grazer.

'Don't be silly,' said Mrs Grazer. 'Only cows say "Moo".'

After the Purée of Spinach, Mrs Grazer bought some Mixed Young

Vegetables and tried them on Maisie the following day. Maisie gollopped them down.

'Maa,' she said.

'Did you hear that?' cried Mrs Grazer. 'She said "More"!'

'It sounded like "Maa" to me,' said Mr Grazer.

'Don't be silly,' said Mrs Grazer. 'Only sheep say "Maa".'

Time passed, and though Maisie Grazer still turned her little nose up at anything to do with meat in it, she seemed to be thriving. Soon, though she still said nothing but 'Moo' or 'Maa', she began to crawl.

The weather was beautiful, and one sunny day Mrs Grazer spread a rug on the little lawn outside and laid

Maisie on it. No sooner had she done so than the front door bell rang.

By the time Mrs Grazer returned from collecting the post, Maisie had crawled to the edge of the rug. But it was not this that nearly made Mrs Grazer's eyes pop out of her head. It was what the baby was doing!

Hastily she snatched her up and hurried indoors.

'What's the matter?' said Mr Grazer when he came back from work that evening. 'You look worried stiff. What's up?'

'It's Maisie,' said Mrs Grazer.

'What about her? She's not ill?'

'No. It's what she was doing, this morning, on the lawn.'

'What was she doing?'

'She was eating grass.'

Mr Grazer laughed.

'Is that all?' he said. 'You had me worried for a moment. Babies are always picking things up and stuffing them in their mouths, you know that. What's a blade or two of grass?'

'It wasn't like that,' said Mrs Grazer in a low voice.

Fuss about nothing, thought Mr Grazer, and he picked up his daughter and carried her out on to the lawn and put her down.

He stood watching, smiling at his wife's groundless fears, but after some moments the smile was replaced by a look of horror, and the colour drained from his cheeks.

'Phone the doctor!' he cried to his wife, scooping Maisie up again. 'Quickly!'

'Now then,' said the doctor when

he arrived, 'who is it that's ill in the Grazer family? The baby looks a picture. Her vegetarian diet seems to be suiting her. You can't have called me out to see her. But you look a bit under the weather, Mr Grazer. And so indeed do you, Mrs Grazer. Which of you is poorly?'

'Neither,' said Mr Grazer.

'It's Maisie,' said Mrs Grazer.

'It's what she's been doing,' they said.

'What's she been doing?' said the doctor.

'Eating grass.'

The doctor laughed.

'That's nothing to worry about,' he said. 'Babies are always picking things up and stuffing them in their mouths. A blade or two of grass won't hurt her.'

'It wasn't a blade or two,' they said.

Fuss about nothing, thought the doctor, and he picked up Maisie and carried her out on to the lawn and put her down.

Without hesitation she dropped her head, opened her mouth, and began to graze. Jaws moving rhythmically, Maisie Grazer crawled slowly along, tearing off the juicy green grass with occasional cries of 'Moo!' or 'Maa!'

until she reached the far edge of the lawn. Behind her stretched a narrow swath of mown ground.

Mrs Grazer ran to pick the baby up and wipe the green stains from her mouth.

'You see, Doctor?' she said.

The doctor nodded.

'Ever known such a thing before, Doctor?' asked Mr Grazer.

The doctor shook his head.

'What d'you think, Doctor?' they said.

'Mr and Mrs Grazer,' said the doctor solemnly, 'I think that your daughter is living up to her name. Such a condition is unknown in medical history. It would appear to me that you are the parents of, and I the doctor attendant on, the world's first grazing baby.'

'But what will it do to her?' they cried.

'That,' said the doctor, 'remains to be seen. Ring me if you need me, otherwise I will call back tomorrow, and in the meantime, wherever you put her, keep off the grass!'

On the following morning the doctor arrived at the Grazers' house very early indeed, so excited was he at this unique case. Would the baby have sicked up its unnatural meal? Would it have a badly upset stomach? Why had the parents not phoned him?

'Why haven't you phoned me?' he said as soon as they opened the door.

'No need,' said Mr Grazer.

'You mean the baby slept the night through?'

'Like a lamb,' said Mrs Grazer.

'Never had a bleat out of her,' said Mr Grazer.

'Amazing!' said the doctor. 'Has she had her breakfast yet?'

'No.'

'Well, I wonder . . . do you think . . . in the interests of medical science . . . that is, seeing that it seems to have done her no harm . . . look here, would you consider, while I'm here, putting her out on the lawn again?'

So they did, and once again Maisie Grazer lowered her little head and opened her little mouth and with her sharp little teeth grazed another swath across the lawn.

'Remarkable!' said the doctor. 'As a matter of interest, just for the record, how many teeth has she?'

'Six,' said Mrs Grazer proudly.

'Imagine!' said the doctor. They

walked back to the house, passing the garden shed in which Mr Grazer kept his lawn-mower.

'Tell you what,' said the doctor, pointing at it. 'Once she's got all thirty-two, you won't need that again.'

And how right he was.

Once Maisie Grazer was old enough, there was never any further need for her father to mow the lawn on a Saturday morning. He could sit in his deckchair with his paper and a cup of coffee, while his daughter did the work. Like all babies she progressed from crawling to toddling to walking to running, but to graze of course she must needs revert to crawling, and by the time she was ten or eleven she could cut the whole lawn in one go. Working methodically from

side to side, she left it as neatly pat-
terned with parallel stripes as the most
expensive machine.

Meat, you will not be surprised to
hear, Maisie Grazer never touched,
but though grass remained her
favourite food, her remarkable powers
of digestion allowed her to eat any
greenstuff raw.

At mealtimes in the Grazer household the father and mother would sit down at table in the normal manner, while out in the garden Maisie would chew on a cabbage or two or munch on a lettuce for lunch.

Sometimes the family doctor, passing on his rounds, would stop his car to look through the fence and smile in smug self-satisfaction at the sight of Maisie among the greenstuff.

'May I live long enough,' he would say to himself, 'to see how her children turn out.'

And he did, for when she was twenty-one, Maisie Grazer married and changed her name, though not her habits. Indeed the honeymoon (in the spring, when the young grass is at its tenderest) was spent in the rich grazing lands of the West Country, where the indulgent young husband could lie at ease and watch his bride, as on hands and knees she munched her way across a field of clover, uttering muffled 'Moos' or 'Maas'.

And a year or so later, Maisie herself became a mother.

How anxiously and with what interest did Mr and Mrs Grazer watch the progress of their grandson, especially when he was first offered solid foods.

As indeed did the old family doctor.

But greatly to the relief of the grandparents and much to the disappointment of the medical man, the baby gollopped down liver-and-bacon or minced beef or lamb casserole, but would not look at Purée of Spinach or Mixed Young Vegetables, and never – throughout his life indeed

– could be persuaded to eat cabbage
or lettuce. He just loved meat, all
sorts of meat and lots of it.

As for grass, that was for him
something to be crawled on, toddled
on, walked on, run on, but not – ever
– eaten.

But then of course he wasn't a
Grazer.

Oh sorry – I forgot to tell you that
the man Maisie married was called
Butcher. Not that he was one of
course, but then you don't expect a
name to *mean* anything, do you?

# Banger

Steven did love sausages!

To say that they were his favourite food was not enough. Steven had sausages all the time. He had them for breakfast, lunch, tea and supper. He had big sausages, short fat ones and long thin ones, pork sausages, beef sausages, Cumberland sausages, chipolatas, saveloys, salami and frankfurters. He ate them fried, boiled, baked, grilled or smoked, hot or cold. And it wasn't simply that Steven had sausages for every meal, every day of every week of every year – oh no, it was more than that. He had sausages with everything he ate.

At breakfast time he would put cornflakes and sugar and milk on a sausage, then eat a sausage with bacon and eggs, and then slice a sausage down the middle and spread each half with butter and jam. You can guess what Steven always began with at lunch and at supper, but for afters he might have rice pudding and sausage, sausage and custard, sausage dumplings with treacle, or perhaps best of all, a vanilla ice-cream cornet with a sausage stuck in the top of it. As for tea, well there were always sausages on hot buttered toast, and perhaps chocolate éclairs with a sausage on each, or just simply sausage-meat sandwiches. And of course Steven never stirred his tea with a spoon if there was a sausage handy.

'Don't you think,' said Steven's father one day (it was funny, he hated sausages), 'that you ought to put Steven on a diet? Or at least make him give up those . . . things?' ( He could not bring himself to say the word.)

'Oh I couldn't,' said Steven's mother from the cooker. 'He does love sausages.'

She turned a row of chipolatas on to their other sides.

Steven's father frowned.

'Have you noticed,' he said, 'what the boy's beginning to look like?' and he went out of the room.

Now most babies do look a bit like sausages when they're very small, but, as they grow bigger, arms and legs and necks begin to stick out of them more, and their bodies are not so plump. This had never happened with Steven. Rather than growing less like a sausage, he had grown more like one.

Steven's mother looked carefully at her son as he rolled into the kitchen. I see what his father means, she thought. Steven's arms and legs weren't really noticeable compared with the size of his body. And he had no neck to speak of, but his head sat on the end of it just like that bit that sometimes comes out of the end of a sausage, she realized. But it was the look of his skin that suddenly worried her. How stretched it was, how brown, how shiny, how greasy! She watched him chopping chipolatas over his porridge.

'Steven,' she said. 'Don't you think three's enough to start with?'

'No,' he said, chopping up a fourth.

'One of these days you'll burst,' she said nervously.

'Like a sausage does,' asked Steven, 'if you forget to stick a fork in it?'

'Yes,' said his mother. 'It gives a little squeak, and a little gurgle, and a little bang.'

'Got my eggs ready?' said Steven with his mouth full. 'I'm hungry.'

Wearily, his mother turned back to the frying-pan.

Two eggs on fried bread and three rashers of bacon (and of course more of Steven's favourite food) followed the chipolatas-and-porridge, and he was just dipping a big pork sausage into the honey-pot when the phone rang in the hall.

While his mother was talking, she

thought that there was a kind of groaning noise coming from the kitchen. She put the phone down and listened.

'Mum!' cried Steven. 'Stick a fork in me! Quick!'

And then she heard a big squeak, and a big gurgle, and a big BANG!

Steven did *love* sausages.

# Poor Edgar

'Poor Edgar,' said Victoria.

'He was very old,' said Alice.

'What did he die of?' said Helena.

'Just being old, I should think,' said Louise.

'How old was he?' said Beatrice.

The five sisters stood staring at the dead guinea-pig, lying on the floor of his hutch. He looked flat.

'Let me think,' said Victoria, the eldest. 'We got him when I was five and now I'm eleven – that makes him six. That's a long life. No wonder he's died.'

The eyes of Beatrice, the youngest, filled with tears and she gave a loud snorting sob.

'Don't cry, Bee,' said Alice. 'He's all right, he's gone to Heaven.'

'It's not that,' gulped Beatrice. 'It's just . . . I don't want to die.'

'Well, why should you?' said Helena.

'Because I'm six. Vicky said that's a long life.'

'For a guinea-pig, she meant,' said Louise.

Beatrice sniffed and Victoria mopped at her.

'Cheer up,' she said. 'We'll give him a lovely funeral, shall we? I'll dig

the hole, and Alice, you and Helena
make a cross to go on his grave, and
Louise, you take Bee and pick some
flowers.'

Digging the hole, under the weeping willow tree at the bottom of the
garden, took quite a long time. The
spade was a bit big for Victoria and

the job was harder than she'd thought it would be. The earth kept falling back in again, and the others were ready long before she was.

Louise had a posy of forget-me-nots ('because we won't,' she said) and Beatrice had picked a lot of dandelion flowers ('because he liked them') and Alice and Helena had made a cross out of two bits of board. On it Alice had written with a felt marker

EDGAR
AGED 6
R.I.P.

'What does R.I.P. mean?' said Beatrice.

'It's what you put on graves,' they said.

'It means "Rest in Peace",' said Victoria, leaning on her spade.

'We ought to have put "Rest in Peace Edgar",' said Alice, and she changed it to R.I.P.E.

Victoria dug out a last spadeful.

'Come on,' she said. 'We'll go and fetch him now.'

'I want to carry him,' said Alice.

'No, me,' said Helena.

'Why can't I?' said Louise.

Beatrice's eyes filled with tears.

'What's the matter now?' they said.

'I don't want to.'

'Don't want to what?'

'Carry him.'

'Well, you needn't,' said Victoria, getting out of the hole. 'The rest of us will be the pall-bearers.'

'What's a pall-bearer?' said Alice and Helena and Louise.

'Someone who carries the coffin.'

'But we haven't got a coffin.'

'Nor we have. That's the next thing to do. We'll find a box and put Edgar in it, and then the four of us can hold a corner each.'

'What about me?' said Beatrice.

'You can be the undertaker and walk behind the coffin.'

Beatrice sniffed.

'I don't want to be the undertaker,' she said.

'Well, what do you want then?'

'I want to be the overtaker.'

'Oh, all right,' said Victoria. 'Call it what you want.'

'But don't start crying again,' said Alice.

'And dry your eyes,' said Helena.

'And blow your nose,' said Louise.

'Come on,' said Victoria. 'Let's go and see what we can find.'

In the garden shed they found an

apple-box. It had a label on it with pictures of lovely juicy red apples.

'Edgar liked them,' said Beatrice in a voice of deepest gloom.

'Well then, it'll be just right for his coffin,' said Victoria.

'Wonder why it's called a coffin?' said Alice.

'Perhaps,' said Helena, 'because people used to die of having a bad cough.'

'Edgar didn't,' said Louise.

Beatrice's eyes filled with tears again.

At last the funeral procession was ready to start.

They had strewn fresh grass on the bed of the apple-box and laid the body

of Edgar reverently upon it, and nailed on the lid.

Alice closed the door of the empty hutch.

'Shall we be able to have another guinea-pig?' she said.

'Or two perhaps?' said Helena.

'They'd be company for each other,' said Louise.

'They cost an awful lot,' said Victoria.

'I've got 10p,' said Beatrice.

'10p!' said Victoria. 'We'd need more like £10 to get two guinea-pigs. We'll just have to save up, that's all. Now then, are you all ready?'

Solemnly the funeral procession made its way down to the weeping willow tree. The four elder girls each held a corner of the apple-box and the overtaker marched behind them, wearing a kind of black bonnet made from a bin liner. All wore black arm-bands of the same material.

They halted at the graveside and carefully lowered the apple-box. It just fitted into the grave but it was obvious that the hole was much too shallow.

'I'll have to make it deeper,' said Victoria.

They took the coffin out again and she set to work.

Another six inches down the spade clinked upon something. Victoria bent and picked up a small round object.

'What is it?' asked the pall-bearers.

'A coin, I think. It's all covered in muck and stuff.'

'See if there are any more.'

Victoria dug around, but there weren't.

Beatrice gave a sob.

'What's the matter, Bee?' they said.

'Can't we put Edgar in the hole now?' she said. 'I don't like frunerals. They make me very very sad.'

'Oh, all right,' said Victoria. 'It's probably only a 2p piece by the size of it anyway,' and she put the thing in the pocket of her jeans.

Then they lowered the coffin once more into the grave.

'We ought to say something,' said Helena.

'Like "Dust to dust and ashes to ashes",' said Alice.

'Can't we just say "Goodbye, Edgar"?' said Louise.

So they all said it, except Beatrice, whose heart was too full for speech, and then they piled the earth on top of the apple-box, and set on the mound the cross with its inscription

EDGAR
AGED 6
R.I.P.E.

and arranged the forget-me-nots and the dandelion flowers around it.

'Edgar has died,' said the girls' mother to her husband when he arrived home from work. 'They gave him a splendid funeral.'

They all went down to the grave, and their father read the inscription on the cross.

'Well, he did live to a ripe old age,' he said.

Beatrice snorted, and Victoria, reaching into her pocket for a handkerchief, suddenly remembered the coin she had found.

She brought it out.

'Look, Dad,' she said. 'I found this when I was digging. What d'you think it is?'

'Let's take it indoors and clean it up a bit,' her father said.

As he was doing so, he suddenly let out a whistle of amazement.

'This is a gold coin!' he said, and when he had scraped at it a bit more,

'It's a guinea!'

'Is that what you use for buying guinea-pigs?' asked Beatrice.

'You could buy an awful lot of them with this, I should think. Guineas must be quite valuable because they stopped making them ages ago, nearly two hundred years, I should think. Let's see if we can make out the date on it. Yes, here it is. 1815. The year of the battle of Waterloo! I'll take it in to that coin-dealer in town tomorrow and get it valued.'

The five girls were all waiting at the gate when their father arrived home the following evening.

'Did you get it valued?' they said.

'Yes.'

'Is it enough to buy two guinea-pigs?' said Victoria.

'What would they cost?'

'About ten pounds.'

'It's worth much more than that.'

'Twenty pounds?' said Alice.

'No, more.'

'Fifty?' said Helena.

'More than that.'

'A hundred pounds,' said Louise. 'It couldn't be worth more than a hundred pounds.'

'The coin dealer,' said her father slowly, 'has offered to buy your

Waterloo guinea for . . . five hundred pounds!'

'Wow!' shouted all the girls. Even Beatrice was beaming broadly.

'And just think,' their father said. 'None of this would have happened if Edgar hadn't died.'

Beatrice's face began to crumple.

'Oh, Dad,' murmured Victoria. 'You shouldn't have said that.'

'Poor Edgar!' howled Beatrice. 'Poor poor Edgar!'

# The Ghost at Codlin Castle

# Contents

The Ghost at Codlin Castle     207

Baldilocks and the Six Bears     225

The Alien at 7B     243

The Adorable Snowman     263

The Message     281

Who Killed Percy Fussell?     295

# The Ghost at Codlin Castle

'Gran,' said Peter as his grandmother was tucking him up in bed, 'd'you believe in ghosts?'

'Oh yes,' said his grandmother.

'So d'you know a good ghost story to tell me?'

'Now?'

'Yes.'

'All right.'

*

Like a great many ghosts (said Gran), Sir Anthony Appleby was wary of people. It wasn't that they could do him any harm. That had been done ages ago. It was the fuss they made when they came upon him, in the winding corridors and steep stone stairways of Codlin Castle.

Some screamed and ran, some stood rooted to the spot, trembling and ashen-faced, some fainted. But no one ever said a kind word to him. In fact, no one had spoken a word of any kind to him since his death in 1588. In time past, things had not been so bad, for then the only inhabitants of Codlin Castle had been the Appleby family and their servants; all were quite used to the ghost of Sir Anthony, and though they may not have spoken to him, at least they were no trouble to him.

Nowadays things were different for the Appleby fortunes had dwindled over the centuries, until finally one of Sir Anthony's descendants had been forced to sell the family seat.

Now it was known as the Codlin Castle Hotel, where well-to-do folk came to stay, to sleep in canopied four-posters and to eat rich meals in the medieval Banqueting Hall. Sir Anthony kept bumping into them in the corridors and stairways, and all of them, it seemed, were frightened of ghosts.

'A fellow can't get any peace these days,' said Sir Anthony grumpily (like all ghosts, he talked to himself a great deal). 'One look at me and they lose their heads,' and then he allowed himself a smile, for though dressed in the costume of his age – doublet and hose, flowing cloak, high ruffed collar, sword by his side – he was, as always, carrying his head underneath one arm.

For three hundred and forty-two years he had carried it thus, ever since that fateful day when, as one of her courtiers, he had accompanied Queen Elizabeth on a visit to her fleet at Tilbury.

On the dockside there was a large puddle, and the Queen stopped before it.

'Your cloak, Sir Anthony,' she said.

Sir Anthony hesitated.

'Majesty?' he said.

'I may have the heart and stomach of a king,' said Queen Elizabeth, 'but I have the feet of a weak and feeble woman and I don't want to get them wet. Cast your cloak upon yonder puddle.'

'But Your Majesty,' said Sir Anthony Appleby, 'it is a brand-new cloak and it will get all muddy,' at which the Queen ordered that he be taken straight away to the Tower of London and there beheaded, while Sir Walter Raleigh hastily threw down his own cloak.

The years and indeed the centuries slipped by. One sultry summer's night in 1930, the stable clock was striking

twelve as the ghost made his way along a stone-flagged passageway in the West Wing, his head tucked underneath his left arm. This was how he usually carried it, to leave his sword-arm free, though sometimes he changed sides for the head was quite heavy. Once, a couple of hundred years ago, he had tried balancing it on top of his neck, just for fun, but this had not been a success. A serving-wench had come

upon him suddenly in the castle kit-
chens, making him jump so that the
head fell off and rolled along the
floor, at which the wretched girl, a
newcomer, had died of fright.

Remembering this incident as the
twelfth stroke sounded, Sir Anthony
stopped opposite a tall cheval-glass
standing in the passage, and taking

up his head with both hands, set it carefully above the great ruffed collar.

'A fine figure of a man,' he remarked to his reflection, 'though I say it myself,' and, pressing his palms against his ears to keep the head steady, he turned this way and that, the better to admire himself. He could not therefore hear the approach of soft footsteps, but suddenly saw, beside his own reflection, that of a small girl in pink pyjamas.

'Hello,' she said. 'Who are you?'

So startled was Sir Anthony that he almost dropped his head.

'My . . . my name is . . . is Sir Anthony Appleby,' he stammered, turning to face the child. 'And who, pray, are you, young miss?'

'I'm Biffy,' said the small girl. 'It's short for Elizabeth.'

That name again, thought Sir Anthony, but at least someone's spoken to me at last.

'Why aren't you in bed?' he said.

'Too hot,' said Biffy. 'I couldn't sleep. Why aren't you?'

'Oh, I never sleep,' said Sir Anthony. 'I'm a ghost, you see.'

'What fun,' said Biffy. 'How long have you been dead?'

'Three hundred and forty-two years.'

'Oh. So that's why you're wearing

those funny clothes.'

'Yes.'

'Why have you got your hands pressed to your ears? Have you the earache?'

'No, no,' said Sir Anthony. 'Ghosts can't feel pain. It's about the only advantage of being one.'

'Then why are you holding your head?' said Biffy.

Oh dear, thought the ghost. If I take off my head, the child will scream or faint or even die of fright. And I do so want her to say a kind word to me. One kind word and I'm sure I could rest in peace at long last, instead of having to trudge round these winding corridors and steep stone stairways for the rest of my death.

'Look,' he said. 'If I tell you a secret, will you promise faithfully not to scream or faint or die of fright?'

'I promise.'

'Well, you see, when I died, it was in a rather unusual way. I mean, it

was common enough then, but they don't do it nowadays.'

'What did they do to you?'

'They executed me. They cut off my head. That's why I'm holding it like this now. I'm just balancing it, you see. It's not attached.'

'What fun,' said Biffy. 'Take it off.'

The ghost's face wore a very worried expression.

'You promised not to scream or faint or die of fright, remember?' he said.

'Yes,' said Biffy. 'Don't worry.'

So Sir Anthony Appleby removed his head, holding it carefully by its long hair, and tucked it under his arm.

The small girl in the pink pyjamas clapped her hands in delight.

'That's wonderful!' she said, and

at these words a broad grin of pleasure spread over the bearded features.

'Oh, Sir Anthony Appleby,' said Biffy. 'You really are the nicest ghost in the whole wide world!' and because she was just the right height, she gave him a kiss on the top of his head.

Immediately the ghost of Codlin Castle vanished.

Biffy looked all round, but there was no sign of him.

She looked in the cheval-glass, but saw only her own reflection, standing there in her pink pyjamas.

So she went back to bed.

\*

'Is that the end of the story?' said Peter.

'Yes, I suppose it is,' said his grandmother. 'Except that from then onward, nobody at the Codlin Castle Hotel ever saw the ghost of Sir Anthony Appleby again.'

'Because he was at peace at last, you mean?'

'Yes.'

'Because the girl said a kind word to him?'

'Yes.'

'Gran,' said Peter. 'Your name's Elizabeth, isn't it?'

'Yes. But when I was little, I was always called Biffy.'

# Baldilocks
# and the
# Six Bears

There was once a magic forest full of
fine tall trees.

In it lived not only animals, but –
because it was a magic forest – fairies
and pixies and elves and goblins.
Some of the goblins were full of mis-
chief and some of the elves were
rather spiteful, but on the whole, the
fairy people were a happy lot. All
except one.

He was a hobgoblin, quite young, not bad-looking; he might even have been thought handsome except for one thing.

He hadn't a hair on his head.

Someone – probably an elf – had named him Baldilocks, and that was what everyone called him.

Baldilocks had never had a great deal of hair, and what he did have had gradually fallen out, till now he had none at all.

How sad he was. How he envied
all the other fairy people their fine
locks and tresses, each time they met,
at the full moon.

In a clearing among the trees was
a huge fairy-ring, and in the middle
of this ring sat the wisest fairy of
them all. She was known as the
Queen of the Forest.

As usual, everyone laughed when
Baldilocks came into the fairy-ring.

'Baldilocks!' someone – probably

an elf — would shout, and then the pixies would titter and the elves would snigger and the goblins would chuckle and the fairies would giggle. All except one.

She was a little red-haired fairy, not specially beautiful but with such a kindly face. She alone did not laugh at the bald hobgoblin.

One night, when everyone was teasing poor Baldilocks as usual, the Queen of the Forest called for silence. Then she said to Baldilocks, 'Would you like to grow a fine head of hair?'

'Oh, I would, Your Majesty!' cried the hobgoblin. 'But how do I go about it?'

'Ask a bear,' said the Queen of

the Forest, and not a word more would she say.

The very next morning Baldilocks set out to find a bear. It did not take him long. He came to a muddy pool, and there was a big brown bear, catching frogs.

'Excuse me,' said Baldilocks. 'Could you tell me how to grow a fine head of hair?'

The brown bear looked carefully at the hobgoblin. He knew that the only way a bald person can grow hair is by rubbing bear's grease into his scalp. But he wasn't going to say that, because he knew that the only way to get bear's grease is to kill a bear and melt him down.

He picked up a pawful of mud.

'Rub this into your scalp,' said the brown bear.

So Baldilocks took the sticky mud

and rubbed it on his head. It was full
of wriggling things and it smelt
horrid. But it didn't make one single
hair grow.

The next bear Baldilocks met was a big black one. It was robbing a wild-bees' nest.

'Excuse me,' said Baldilocks. 'Could you tell me how to grow a fine head of hair?'

The black bear looked carefully at the hobgoblin. He too knew the only way for a bald person to grow hair. He pulled out a pawful of honey-comb.

'Rub this into your scalp,' said the black bear.

So Baldilocks took the honey and rubbed it on his head. It was horribly sticky and it had several angry bees in it that stung him. But it didn't make one single hair grow.

The third bear that Baldilocks met was a big gingery one, that was digging for grubs in a nettle patch.

Baldilocks asked his question

again, and the ginger bear, after looking carefully at him, pulled up a
pawful of nettles and said, 'Rub these
into your scalp.'

So Baldilocks took the nettles and
rubbed them on his head. They stung
him so much that his eyes began to
water, but they didn't make one
single hair grow.

The fourth bear that Baldilocks
came across, a big chocolate-coloured
one, was digging out an ants' nest,
and by way of reply to the hobgoblin,
he handed him a pawful of earth that
was full of ants.

When Baldilocks rubbed it on his
head, the ants bit him so hard that
the tears rolled down his face, but
they didn't make one single hair grow.
Baldilocks found the fifth bear by the
side of a river that ran through the
forest. It was a big old grey bear, and

it was eating some fish that had been
left high and dry on the bank by a
flood. They looked to have been dead
for a long time, and when Baldilocks's
question had been asked and answered, and he had rubbed the rotten
fish on his head, they made it smell
perfectly awful. But, once again, they
didn't make one single hair grow.

Baldilocks had just about had enough. What with the mud and the honey and all the stings and bites and the stink of the fish, he almost began to hope that he wouldn't meet another bear. But he did.

It was a baby bear, a little golden one, and it was sitting in the sun doing nothing.

'Excuse me,' said Baldilocks. 'Could you tell me how to grow a fine head of hair?'

The baby bear looked fearfully at the hobgoblin. He knew, although he was so young, that the only way for a bald person to grow hair is by rubbing bear's grease into his scalp. And he knew, although he was so young, that the only way to get bear's grease is to kill a bear and melt him down.

He did not answer, so Baldilocks, to

encourage him, said, 'I expect you'll tell me to rub something into my scalp.'

'Yes,' said the baby bear in a small voice.

'What?'

'Bear's grease,' said the baby bear in a small voice.

'Bear's grease?' said Baldilocks. 'How do I get hold of that?'

'You have to kill a bear,' said the baby bear in a whisper, 'and melt him down.'

'Oh!' said Baldilocks. 'Oh no!' he said.

When next the fairy people met, and the hobgoblin came into the fairy-ring, someone – probably an elf – shouted 'Baldilocks!' and everyone laughed, except the little red-haired fairy.

The Queen of the Forest called for silence. Then she said to Baldilocks, 'You haven't grown any hair. Didn't you ask a bear?'

'I asked six, Your Majesty,' said Baldilocks, 'before I found out that what I need is bear's grease, and to get that I would have to kill a bear and melt him down.'

'That might be difficult,' said the Queen of the Forest, 'but perhaps you could kill a little one?'

She smiled as she spoke, because she knew, being the wisest fairy of them all, that high in a nearby tree a small golden bear sat listening anxiously.

'I couldn't do such a thing,' said Baldilocks. 'I'd sooner stay bald and unhappy.'

Up in the tree, the baby bear hugged himself silently.

After the others had gone away, Baldilocks still sat alone in the fairy-ring. At least he thought he was alone, till he looked round and saw that the little red-haired fairy with the kindly face was still sitting there too.

'I think,' she said, 'that bald people are much the nicest.'

'You do?' said Baldilocks.

'Yes. So you mustn't be unhappy any more. If you are, you will make me very sad.'

Baldilocks looked at her, and to his eyes it seemed that she didn't simply have a kindly face, she was beautiful.

He smiled the happiest of smiles.

'You mustn't be sad,' he said. 'That's something I couldn't bear.'

# The Alien at 7B

At first sight the Alien looked like a sausage, an uncooked sausage. It was pinkish, its skin was shiny, and, like a sausage, it seemed long and thick and fat, all at the same time.

There were differences however.

To begin with, it was the size of a very large pig (if you can imagine a legless, earless pig), and then again, unlike any sausage, it had a pair of small round eyes and, between them, a mouth shaped like the opening of a letter-box. What's more, the Alien had a second pair of eyes and a second mouth at the other end of its body, so that there was no knowing which was its front and which was its rear.

It lay, motionless, on the lawn in the small front garden of 7B, Marine View, Littleton-on-Sea.

Though the round eyes and the oblong slits were open, the creature was so still that a cheeky sparrow hopped up to one of the letter-box mouths and, cocking his head on one side, peered in.

Suddenly there was a sound like a sharply indrawn breath, and the bird was sucked from sight. A slight tremor rippled down the body of the Alien, and then, after a moment, a little cloud of feathers blew out of the other mouth.

For a while, nothing else happened. It was early in the morning and few people were about yet in the little seaside town. The curtains of

the houses in Marine View were still drawn, and the only inhabitant of 7B to be seen was a large ginger tom-cat, which emerged from a flap in the back door and sauntered round to the front garden.

At sight of the Alien, he stopped dead in his tracks, ears pricked, tail twitching. But seeing no movement, the cat inched forward and cautiously sniffed at the side of the fat pink body. Then, curious, he moved to one end of the thing, where a few brown feathers lay on the ground.

Once again there came that sharp sucking noise, and into the expanding oblong of the letter-box slit went the cat, tail first. For a fraction of a second, his round astonished face

looked its last upon the world, and then he was gone. Once more a ripple ran along the great sausage shape, and then the mouth at the other end blew out a little parcel of ginger fur.

Further up Marine View, the chinking of bottles told that the milkman was on his way, and before long he opened the wrought-iron gate of 7B and came in with three pints of

Gold Top. He had placed them on the highest step outside the front door and turned away before he noticed the strange object lying on the lawn, feathers at one end of it, fur at the other.

'People chuck their rubbish anywhere nowadays,' said the milkman, who was rather short-sighted, and he shut the gate and climbed back into his electric cart.

No sooner had he gone than the Alien moved.

To anyone watching, it would have seemed a mystery how the sausage shape could slowly slide along the ground without any legs. In fact, it was simply done. It merely sucked in air through one mouth and blew it out through the other. By this process, it had jetted the many millions of miles from its native planet to land, quite by chance, in Littleton-on-Sea.

Now it slid forward to the steps of 7B, its leading pair of eyes fixed upon the milk bottles.

'Schloop!' and one pint vanished

into the mouth-slit.

'Schloop! Schloop!' and the others followed.

Silently the Alien slid back to its original position. Deep within the shiny pink body could be heard a tiny tinkling noise, and then from the rear mouth came a little shower of broken glass and three gold bottle-tops.

At that moment the front door of

7B half opened, and a man in dressing-gown and slippers peered round it, yawning and rubbing his eyes.

Automatically he bent to pick up the milk bottles before he realized there were none.

'The milkman hasn't been,' he called to someone inside the house.

'Yes, he has,' a woman's voice replied. 'I heard him.'

'Well, there's no milk on the doorstep.'

'Nip down the road and catch him then. He can't be far off.'

'I'm not going out in my dressing-gown and slippers.'

'Oh, all right, I'll send Debbie then,' the woman said. 'Debbie!'

'Yes, Mum?' said a girl's voice.

'Are you dressed?'

'Yes, Mum.'

'Pop down the road, there's a good girl, and get three pints. The milkman's forgotten us.'

'OK, Mum.'

The moment Debbie came out through the front door of 7B, she saw the Alien. Not that either of her parents could have failed to see it, had they come out into the garden. It was too big and strange-looking for anyone but a short-sighted milkman to miss. But they would have had no idea what it was. Debbie knew immediately.

Not for nothing had she read every science-fiction book she could lay her hands on, watched every cartoon, seen every film about creatures from outer space. There was nothing she didn't know about Aliens, and this was one, beyond the shadow of a doubt!

But was it friendly?

Keeping well away from it, in case it wasn't, she said in the politest of tones, 'Welcome to our planet.'

The Alien stared unblinkingly at her with its round eyes, but no sound came from the oblong mouth-slit.

'Look,' said Debbie. 'I've just got to fetch some milk. Don't go away.'

She went out of the gate, and, turning for another look, could see that on the other end of the great pink sausage-shaped body was a second pair of eyes and a second mouth.

Maybe I was talking to the wrong end, she thought, so she repeated her greeting, but again there was no reply.

When Debbie came hurrying back with three more bottles of milk, she was in such a rush to hand them over and return to examine the Alien more closely that she forgot to shut the front gate.

This was the opportunity for which 7A's dog had been waiting.

Every day 7B's ginger tom would sit on the dividing wall and make catty remarks, and every day the dog, a fat, bad-tempered terrier with a brass-studded collar, would hope against hope that some time or other the gate of 7B would be left open.

Then, with luck, he would catch that cat unawares and make mincemeat of him.

Now, when the dog dashed in, there was no ginger tom to be seen, but only a strange thing that looked like a giant pink sausage. The terrier advanced upon it, barking and growling.

Debbie came back out of the front door just in time to hear the barking drowned by that dreadful schlooping noise, and to see the wretched dog disappear head first into the Alien.

Again the bloated body shuddered a little, and then from the other mouth a brass-studded collar came flying out.

'This Alien,' said Debbie, 'is definitely not friendly,' and even as she spoke, she saw it begin to slide across the grass towards her.

She dashed inside 7B and slammed the door.

'Debbie,' said her mother as the family sat at breakfast. 'Why are you gobbling your food like that?'

'It's Saturday, you know,' said her

father from behind his newspaper. 'No school today. What's the hurry?'

'There's an Alien in the front garden,' said Debbie.

'E.T. I suppose,' said her father.

'No,' said Debbie. 'This is an un-friendly Alien.'

'I expect it'll wait for you,' her mother said. 'No need to bolt your food.'

It'll wait for me all right, thought Debbie, and it'll bolt me if I'm not mistaken. And Mum. And Dad. And probably everyone in Littleton-on-Sea. I must deal with it. But how?

Let's see – it sucks things in one end and blows things out the other. Of course! That's how it propels itself, that's how it got here from outer space. I've got to persuade it to take off again before it does any more damage. But how?

It was while Debbie was washing up — one of her jobs on a Saturday — that the answer came to her. Because she was thinking hard about how to deal with the Alien, she absent-mindedly squirted much too much washing-up liquid into the bowl and it rose up in a cloud of soap bubbles.

That's it, thought Debbie! Fill the Alien full of that stuff, and it'll float away, like it or not.

Quickly she finished the breakfast things, and took a new jumbo-sized container of washing-up liquid from the kitchen cupboard.

Stealthily she made her way to the front door and peeped out through the flap of the letter-box.

To her surprise, she could see nothing.

Then all of a sudden the horrid truth burst upon Debbie. Outside, the Alien had one of its mouths, a mouth shaped exactly like the opening of a letter-box, pressed against the one in the front door of 7B!

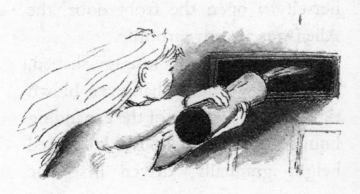

Quick as a flash, Debbie thrust the nozzle of the washing-up container into the flap, and as she did so, she heard that dreadful schlooping noise and felt a terrible suction pull her flat against the door. For a moment she struggled madly, face pressed to the wood, feet kicking helplessly, and then it was over and she was standing in the hall, holding a jumbo-sized container of washing-up liquid that contained nothing. It was empty, sucked dry.

By the time Debbie had nerved herself to open the front door, the Alien was already airborne.

Pink, pig-sized, sausage-shaped, its skin now shinier than ever, blown tight by the pressure of the expanding liquid within its body, it gained height gradually, driven first one way, then another, as from either mouth came spasmodic bursts of soapy bubbles, while its two pairs of round eyes seemed ready to burst.

Up above 7B it rose, up above Marine View, up above Littleton-on-Sea, until at last it was lost from sight among the clouds.

Carefully Debbie set about tidying up the front garden. Thoughtfully she picked up some feathers, a parcel of what looked like ginger fur, a lot of broken glass, three gold bottle-tops, and a brass-studded collar, and

put them in the dustbin. Then she dropped the empty washing-up liquid container in as well. Then she went indoors.

'Mum! Dad!' she said. 'It's all right now. The Alien's gone.'

'You and your Aliens!' her father said.

Her mother poured some milk into a saucer.

'Debbie, I do wish you'd stop imagining things,' she said. 'Here, take this out for the cat.'

# The Adorable Snowman

In a snow-cave, half-way up Mount Everest, sat a family of yetis. There were three of them, father, mother and son, all covered in long, reddish hair.

Daddyeti was much taller than a man.

Mummyeti was the same size as a man.

Babyeti was very young, only about six months old, in fact, but still he was as big as the average six-year-old boy. But unlike the average six-year-old boy, Babyeti had never met any other living creature but Daddyeti and Mummyeti. Except for

a few birds, that is. Otherwise
nobody had disturbed the peace of
Mount Everest during that first half
year of his life.

However, that morning Babyeti got a big surprise.

'Can I go out and play, Mum?' he asked.

'All right,' said Mummyeti, 'but watch out for avalanches.'

'And don't go falling down any crevasses,' said Daddyeti.

But Babyeti had gone only a few yards from the mouth of the cave when he saw, far below, a line of little figures showing up blackly against the dazzling whiteness of the snow.

'Mum! Dad!' he called, and when his parents came out to see what was the matter, he pointed down to the distant figures.

'Whatever are those?' he said.

Daddyeti gave a grunt of annoyance.

'Humans!' he said angrily.

Mummyeti sighed.

'What a nuisance,' she said. 'Why can't they stay where they belong?'

'We haven't had any for nearly a year,' said Daddyeti.

'But what are humans, Dad?' asked Babyeti.

'Well,' said Daddyeti, 'I suppose they are a sort of monkey, except that they don't seem to have any hair on their bodies. They have to wrap themselves in all kinds of stuff to keep warm.'

'But what do they look like?'

'You can't see,' said Mummyeti. 'As well as covering up their bodies and their paws and their heads, they wear round black things they call goggles over their eyes, so that you

can't see their faces. And they're all
tied to one another with long ropes.'

'But why do these humans come
up the mountain?' asked Babyeti.

'To get to the top,' said Daddyeti.

'And do they?'

'Usually. They never did when I was a young yeti, but nowadays they almost always do.'

'And when they've got to the top, what do they do then?'

'Come down again.'

'Oh,' said Babyeti, 'I see . . . d'you think that I could meet one?'

'Certainly not!' said Mummyeti sharply.

'Why not?'

'Because humans have absolutely no respect for yetis. D'you know what they call us? They call us Abominable Snowmen.'

'You mean they'd call Dad an Abominable Snowman?'

'Yes.'

'So you'd be an Abominable Snow-woman?'

'Well, yes, I suppose so.'

'And I'd be an Abominable

Snowbaby?'

'Yes.'

'What does "abominable" mean?'

'It means detestable,' growled Daddyeti.

'And what does that mean?'

'It means hateful,' said Mummy-eti. 'Though why they should hate us, I don't know. We've never done them any harm. Nor has any other yeti.'

'Yet,' said Daddyeti darkly. 'Now

then, inside the cave, both of you, and we'll block up the mouth with snow. Those humans will be up this high by nightfall.'

'Do they stop at night?' said Babyeti.

'Yes. They're frightened of the dark, I think. They get inside little shelters called tents and wait for day-light.'

Babyeti couldn't get to sleep that night. He lay thinking about the

strange humans and wondering why
they thought that yetis were hateful.
I wish I could ask one, he thought.

He lay listening to his parents snor-
ing.

I *will* ask one, he thought sleepily.
I can quickly nip along the mountain-
side and find a human and ask it,
and then be back here before Mum
and Dad notice anything. So very
quietly he burrowed a hole through
the snow that was blocking the cave-
mouth.

The night was quite a still one, and the moon shone brightly on Mount Everest. Babyeti could see, not far below, a number of strange shapes on the steep slope, the tents of which Dad had spoken.

Swiftly and silently Babyeti scrambled down to the nearest one and, cautiously raising the flap, found himself staring at a sleeping human. Its body and its paws and its head were wrapped up, but it wasn't tied to anyone and it didn't have any goggles over its eyes. In fact, it suddenly opened them and stared back at Babyeti.

Then the human gave a gasp of surprise.

'Heavens above!' it said softly. 'The Abominable Snowman!'

'Why do you call me that?' said Babyeti. 'Abominable means detestable and detestable means hateful. What reason have you to hate me?'

'No reason at all, now I come to think of it,' said the human.

'It'd be different,' said Babyeti, 'if I were to do you any harm. But I wouldn't dream of such a thing, and nor would any other yeti. I must say, I think it's a bit unfair to call us abominable.'

'You are absolutely right,' said the human. 'I do apologize. No one could possibly hate you. In fact, I think you're a perfectly lovely little chap.'

'Oh thanks,' said Babyeti.

'What you need,' said the human, 'is a new name. I shall call you the Adorable Snowman.'

'Oh good,' said Babyeti, and he let down the flap of the tent and made his way back to the snow-cave.

When the climbers woke next morning, one of them said to the others, 'I saw a yeti last night. It came to my tent. It spoke to me. It was a perfectly lovely little chap.'

The others looked at one another.

'You've been dreaming,' they said.

When the yetis woke next morning, Babyeti said to his parents, 'I saw a human last night. I went to its tent. I spoke to it. It said I was an Adorable Snowman.'

Daddyeti and Mummyeti looked

at one another.

'You've been dreaming,' they said.

'I haven't. It's true.'

'Now, now,' they said. 'You mustn't tell lies.'

Babyeti grinned.

As if I would, he thought. What an abominable thing to say.

# The Message

'Look!' said Robert to his cousin James. 'There's a bottle coming down!'

The two boys were leaning over the parapet of the stone bridge that spanned the river, and they watched the bottle sailing closer.

It was a clear glass one, with a cork in its neck, and as it passed directly beneath them, James said, 'It's got something in it.'

'It looks like a rolled-up piece of paper,' said Robert.

'A message!' said James.

'Let's get it!' they cried, and they ran off the bridge and down on to the river bank.

The current was sluggish, and the boys had no difficulty in keeping pace with the floating bottle, but it stayed stubbornly out in midstream.

'Let's not bother,' said James, who was a nervous boy by nature and, though he had learned to swim, was still scared of water. 'Let's just leave it.'

Robert, on the other hand, was a bold boy, afraid of nothing.

'Wait a bit,' he said. 'We've got to find out if that is a message inside, and if so, what it says. Maybe someone needs help.'

Just then a motor cruiser came chugging upriver, and after it had passed them, its wake rocked the bottle and moved it a little nearer the bank.

'That's an idea,' Robert said. 'Let's find some big stones and chuck them beyond the bottle and that'll help to wash it in close enough for us to get it.'

James hesitated. I'll probably throw them the wrong side or even hit it and sink it, he thought.

'You do it,' he said. 'I'm not good at throwing like you are.'

'Well, you go and find a long stick or a branch or something,' said Robert. 'Something to hook it out with when I've got it near enough.'

Just so long as he doesn't want me to go in and get that bottle out, said James to himself as he trudged off. That river looks awfully deep. And cold. And brown and mucky. But then he's sure to want to get it out himself, Robert is. I wish I was brave like him.

By the time he got back, carrying a longish branch that he had found, Robert's accurate stone-throwing had brought the bottle much closer to the bank. Better still, it was now lodged in a clump of reeds that stopped it floating on downriver.

'See if you can reach it with this branch,' said James, but it was still too far out.

'I'm going in after it,' Robert said.

'It's too deep,' said James. 'The water will come over the top of your wellies.'

'That's not the end of the world,' said Robert. 'If it was summertime, I'd have swum out after it, but it's a bit too chilly for that,' and he began to wade in.

'Coo, it's muddy at the bottom,'

he said, 'and smelly old mud at that.'

'Be careful, Robert,' James said anxiously. 'You might get stuck.'

'Nearly there,' said Robert, and he lunged forward and grabbed the bottle by its neck. As he did so, he sank a little so that the water filled his wellies.

'You were right, James!' he shouted, laughing. 'But anyway I got it!' and he hurled the bottle up on to the bank.

'Are you all right?' said James.

'Of course.'

'Well, come on out then.'

There was a pause and then Robert said, 'I can't.'

'Why not?'

'My boots are stuck. In the mud.'

'Kick them off.'

'I can't,' said Robert, and suddenly his voice sounded strained. 'I can't get my feet out of them.

They've gone in too far.'

To his horror, James saw that
Robert was now nearly waist-deep.
Even as he watched, he saw that the
water was creeping up. Not only was
Robert stuck in the mud, he was
slowly sinking in it, and the more he
struggled to free his feet, the lower
he sank.

He turned a white face to his cousin on the bank.

'Help me!' he panted. 'James! Help me!'

He's going to drown, thought James. He's going to keep sinking in that horrible river mud, all soft and squelchy like quicksand, until his head goes under. It doesn't matter that he's a strong swimmer, his feet are stuck inside his boots and he can't get them out. And if I go in to try to rescue him, I shall drown too. I'm not even a strong swimmer. Oh, what shall I do?

Afterwards, James never understood how it was that he answered this last question in the way that he did.

Every bit of him said 'Don't go! One drowned is bad enough, why make it two?' and yet the next thing

he knew was that he had kicked off
his wellies and belly-flopped into the

cold, cold water, and was swimming
with the mad, panicky breast-stroke
that was all he could manage.

Afterwards, he couldn't think how
he had found the strength to keep
himself afloat and somehow, Heaven
only knows how, to pull Robert free
from his trapped boots. The distance
back to the safety of dry land was no

more than a few yards, but later it seemed to James like it had been miles, before at last they sat side by side on the bank, exhausted, soaked, and shivering with cold.

Then Robert said slowly, 'You saved my life.'

James gave a sort of nervous giggle.

'You've lost your wellies,' he said. 'You can have one of mine if you like and we'll hop home like they do in three-legged races. Come on, we'd

better get moving.'

'And all for a stupid bottle,' said Robert as they stood up. 'Where is the thing anyway?'

They searched about and found the bottle lying in the long grass.

'Might as well see what's in it,' said Robert.

He pulled out the cork, and with a thin bit of stick, he fished the rolled-up piece of paper out through the neck.

He smoothed it out, and the two cousins each held a corner and scanned it.

Then they looked at one another, in amazement, for this is what was written on it.

# Who Killed
# Percy Fussell?

It all begin when Mr Bishop dug the
goldfish pool.

Up till then, everything in the
garden had been lovely, and Mr and
Mrs Bishop's collection of gnomes
had been one big happy family.

There were five of them, grey-beards all, dressed in brightly coloured smocks and baggy trousers, with floppy caps on their heads and long pointed shoes on their feet.

Mr Bishop liked to go down to the pub of an evening for a glass of beer and a game of dominoes with his cronies, and he had named his gnomes after some of those friends.

There was Bill Stubbs (who

smoked a pipe, just like the real-life
Bill), and Harry Pickett, and Tom
Parsons, and Bob Button who walked
with a stick as the other Bob did, and
Arthur Prendergast.

Mr and Mrs Bishop were very
fond of them all. Each evening, when
Mr Bishop had finished his gardening
and was having a drink with the real
Bill and Harry and Tom and Bob
and Arthur, Mrs Bishop would come

out with a sponge and warm water and detergent, and clean up their namesakes.

Not that the gnomes got very dirty, for of course every time it rained, they had a shower. But quite often birds would perch upon them and weren't too particular what they did. Then Mrs Bishop would go into action, so that when Mr Bishop came home from the pub, all the gnomes were spick and span, each with a permanent broad smile upon his bearded features. There followed a last walk round the garden and a final 'Good-night' to Bill and Harry and Tom and Bob and Arthur, and then Mr and Mrs Bishop would go indoors for cocoa and biscuits and bed. Little did they dream what happened later in the darkness.

How many of you, I wonder, have

ever realized that when night falls,
every garden gnome in the land
comes to life?

Down from their little pedestals
would step the Bishops' five old fellows and stretch and yawn and turn
their heads this way and that to ease
the stiffness caused by standing still
all day. Bill Stubbs would light his
pipe, and then he and Harry and Tom
and Bob, leaning on his walking-stick,
and Arthur Prendergast would take a

stroll around the garden, chatting happily about the day's events.

What a pleasant life they led, until Mr Bishop dug the goldfish pool.

It was something that Mrs Bishop had long wanted.

'It needn't be a big one,' she said to her husband. 'You could easily dig a hole down in the bottom corner by the privet hedge, and you could put one of those plastic liners in it, and we could have water-lilies too, and half a dozen fish or so. We could get everything down at the Garden Centre.'

None of that would have mattered to the gnomes – indeed, it could have been very pleasant for them to sit around the pool on warm nights and dabble their long pointed shoes in the water – if only Mr Bishop had not bought something else at the Garden Centre.

'Oh look!' said Mrs Bishop, as they were leaving it. 'Isn't he lovely!'

Mr Bishop looked and saw that she was pointing at another garden gnome. He was quite a bit bigger than their five, and he was seated cross-legged on a large orange toadstool with white spots. In his hands he held a long fishing-rod with a length of real line attached to it and a real wooden red-and-blue float.

'Can't you just see him, sitting by the edge of the pool with his little

float in the water?' said Mrs Bishop. 'Wouldn't he look nice!'

'I reckon he would,' said Mr Bishop.

So they bought him.

By the end of the day, everything was completed. The liner was fitted in the hole, the water-lilies in their containers placed on the bottom, the pool filled, the goldfish put in.

Finally, while Mrs Bishop stood by, wreathed in smiles, Mr Bishop set the toadstool that bore the large angling gnome beside the rim. The fishing-rod stuck out over the water, the line hung down, the float floated.

'What shall we call him?' said Mrs Bishop.

Mr Bishop looked at the face of the angling gnome. It wore a smug, self-satisfied expression.

'Reminds me of a chap I used to know called Percy Fussell,' he said. 'Ever so keen on fishing, he was, and always boasting about the size of the fish he caught. Proper loud-mouthed bighead, and grumpy with it, though I shouldn't speak ill of the dead. Fell in the river one day and drowned, Percy did. We'll call him Percy Fussell.'

'Should we?' said Mrs Bishop. 'He might fall in the goldfish pool.'

'Well, if he did, he couldn't drown, could he?' said Mr Bishop, and they laughed and said 'Good-night' to Percy Fussell and went indoors.

After dark the five resident gnomes came to life as usual and set out for their walk round the garden. On the previous night, they had come upon the hole dug in the bottom corner by the privet hedge, and wondered what it was for. Now, to their amazement, they could clearly see (for the moon was bright) a goldfish pool. And sitting beside it on a large orange

toadstool with white spots was a very big gnome, holding something in this hands.

Bill Stubbs took his pipe out of his mouth.

'Who's he?' he said.

'Never seen him before,' said Harry Pickett.

'Big chap, isn't he?' said Tom Parsons.

Bob Button pointed with his

walking-stick.

'He's fishing,' he said.

Arthur Prendergast approached the fishing gnome.

'Good evening,' he said politely.

The newcomer spun round on his toadstool.

'Can't you keep your voices down?' he hissed. 'How's a chap expected to catch fish when you lot are making all that row? If it hadn't been for you, I'd have landed one by now, or my name's not Percy Fussell. Why don't you push off?'

If that had been an isolated outburst, things might still have been all right. But it wasn't.

Every time that the Bishops' five gnomes strolled down to the goldfish pool, the smoke from Bill Stubbs's pipe curling in the night air while Bob Button's stick tap-tapped on the path, Percy Fussell would have something unpleasant to say.

At first he only told them to be quiet, but as time passed, he became ruder and ruder, until one night he rounded on them and said in a very angry voice, 'Now listen, you lot. I'm warning you. This is *my* goldfish pool, so in future you just keep away

from it or there'll be trouble, understand?' and he waved his rod at them
in a threatening manner.

'Blooming cheek!' said Arthur
Prendergast as they retreated to the
upper end of the garden.

'Nasty piece of work, that Percy
Fussell,' said Bob Button, gripping
his walking-stick angrily.

'Why shouldn't we go to the
pool?' said Tom Parsons.

'We could if only he wasn't there,'
said Harry Pickett.

Bill Stubbs puffed his pipe.

'If only he wasn't there,' he repeated thoughtfully. 'Now listen to
me, lads . . .'

So it was that on the following night,
a dark and windy one, five shadowy
shapes silently approached the goldfish pool. Bill's pipe was not lit, and

Bob leaned on Arthur Prendergast's shoulder, his walking-stick under his arm so as to make no noise.

Percy Fussell sat fishing, the usual smug, self-satisfied look on his face,

when suddenly there was a rush, and a cry, and a great splash, and then silence. A ring of ripples spread from the centre of the pool, and for a little while, a string of bubbles rose up through the water and burst. Then the surface was still once more.

'Look at this!' called Mr Bishop to his wife next morning, and they stood and stared into the goldfish pool. There at the bottom lay Percy Fussell, still seated on his toadstool, his rod still in his hands, the line leading upwards, the red-and-blue float bobbing on the surface.

'However did that happen?' asked Mrs Bishop.

Mr Bishop fished the gnome out and set him once more on the brink.

'Don't know,' he said. 'Just like the real Percy Fussell. Except that this time there's no harm done.'

Sure enough, the following night, when Bill Stubbs and Harry Pickett and Tom Parsons and Bob Button

and Arthur Prendergast strolled
down to the goldfish pool, there was
Percy Fussell, sitting on his toadstool,
fishing as before. Still as stone he sat,
but for all time now, and never a
word he spoke nor ever would again.

As for Bill and Harry and Tom
and Bob and Arthur, they dabbled
their long pointed shoes in the water
and smiled happily at one another,
confident that no one would ever
know who killed Percy Fussell.